PUFFIN BOOKS

D1100831

The Black Paw

02178

SPY MICE
The Black Paw

HEATHER VOGEL FREDERICK

illustrations by **SALLY WERN COMPORT**

PUFFIN

PUFFIN BOOKS

Published by the Penguin Group
Penguin Books Ltd, 80 Strand, London WC2R 0RL, England
Penguin Group (USA) Inc., 375 Hudson Street, New York, New York 10014, USA
Penguin Group (Canada), 90 Eglinton Avenue East, Suite 700, Toronto,
Ontario, Canada M4P 2Y3 (a division of Pearson Penguin Canada Inc.)
Penguin Ireland, 25 St Stephen's Green, Dublin 2, Ireland
(a division of Penguin Books Ltd)
Penguin Group (Australia), 250 Camberwell Road, Camberwell, Victoria 3124,
Australia (a division of Pearson Australia Group Pty Ltd)
Penguin Books India Pvt Ltd, 11 Community Centre, Panchsheel Park, New
Delhi – 110 017, India
Penguin Group (NZ), cnr Airborne and Rosedale Roads, Albany, Auckland
1310, New Zealand (a division of Pearson New Zealand Ltd)
Penguin Books (South Africa) (Pty) Ltd, 24 Sturdee Avenue, Rosebank,
Johannesburg 2196, South Africa

Penguin Books Ltd, Registered Offices: 80 Strand, London WC2R 0RL, England

www.penguin.com

First published in the USA by Simon & Schuster Books for Young Readers 2005
First published in Puffin Books 2005
1

Set in Stone Serif
Made and printed in England by Clays Ltd, St Ives plc

British Library Cataloguing in Publication Data
A CIP catalogue record for this book is available from the British Library

ISBN 0–141–31986–0

For Cousin Dorothy, who is true blue

CHAPTER 1

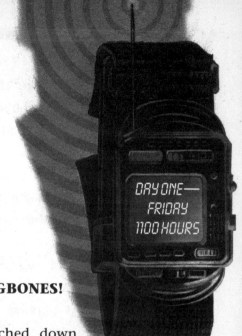

DAY ONE—
FRIDAY
1100 HOURS

"DOGBONES! DOGBONES! DOGBONES!"

Oz Levinson crouched down behind the gleaming gray sports car. He prodded his glasses up the perspiring slope of his nose and squeezed his eyes tightly shut, wishing he were invisible.

"DOGBONES! DOGBONES! DOGBONES!"

Oz covered his ears, but the chant pushed past his hands. It was the sharks again, same as at his old school. Different faces, different names, but the voices were the same. Taunting, teasing voices. Voices out for blood. Or tears, at the very least. And even though the sharks weren't after him this time, Oz's stomach still cramped in familiar knots of panic at the sound.

"DOGBONES! DOGBONES! DOGBONES!"

The sharks were drawing closer now. It wouldn't be long before they discovered his hiding place. Oz opened one eye and looked around in desperation for a better place to conceal himself. Running was pointless. He was fat; he was slow; they'd catch him for sure—even though he wasn't the "Dogbones" they were after. One prey was as good as another when the sharks caught the sour scent of fear.

Oz's gaze settled on the sports car beside him. The James Bond Aston Martin DB5 was the International Spy Museum's most popular exhibit, and he'd spent most of the morning's school field trip glued to its side. Its elegant lines and impressive array of modifications drew him like a magnet. Dual ram bumpers. Bulletproof glass. Armored panels. Gun ports. Tear gas. It was sleek. It was dangerous. Just like he, Oz Levinson, would be someday when he was a secret agent.

"DOGBONES! DOGBONES! DOGBONES!"

The sharks were almost on top of him. Oz huddled lower and drew a shaky breath. The Aston Martin had an emergency oxygen system. He could use a little bit of that right about now. Either that or the DB5's smoke screen. A smoke screen would give him the perfect cover he needed to escape. A smoke screen—

"Hey, whadda we got here?"

Oz flinched as the bubble of his daydream burst. He looked up and poked nervously at his glasses again. Over him loomed Jordan Scott and Sherman "Tank" Wilson. Unlike his last school in San Francisco, where sixth grade thugs like Jordan and Tank were shipped off to middle school, Chester B. Arthur Elementary in Washington, D.C., kept them around one more year. One more year to torture the younger kids and make lives like his miserable.

Reluctantly, Oz rose to his feet. Jordan stepped forward and jabbed him in the belly. "Seen Dogbones around anywhere, Fatboy?"

"Uh," said Oz, stalling for time. They were after his fifth grade classmate Delilah Bean, better known as "Dogbones" thanks to a pair of exceedingly skinny legs and what passed for wit amongst the sharks.

He swallowed nervously and stared at Jordan. The older boy was lumbering right up the food chain toward adolescence. A thatch of shaggy dark hair partially obscured his narrow face, which sprouted a scattering of whiskers and acne. Oz studied the constellation of pimples on his tormentor's chin and wondered what to say. In fact, he knew exactly where Delilah Bean was hiding—in the museum's secret passageway through the ductwork overhead—but he had no

intention of ratting her out. Not to the likes of Jordan and Tank.

On the other hand, if he told them where Delilah Bean was hiding, maybe they'd let him off easy. Maybe they'd leave him alone.

Or maybe they'd even let him become one of them. A shark.

The thought was enormously tempting. Oz was so tired of always wishing he were invisible. Of always trying to stay off the radar screen. Maybe this was finally his chance. He didn't even have to say anything. All he had to do was point.

"C'mon, Blubberbutt, you know who I'm talking about." Jordan was growing impatient. "Skinny legs, skinny little braids. I'll bet you've seen her."

Oz started to raise his finger toward the ceiling, then hesitated. What would James Bond do if he were here? James Bond was Oz's hero. He'd watched all the 007 movies at least a zillion times. Nothing ever rattled the world's most famous spy. He never caved in to pressure, never lost his cool. The sharks wouldn't stand a chance around James Bond. The British secret agent would make mincemeat out of a pimpleton like Jordan Scott.

"Are you deaf as well as blind?" Tank, a beefy redhead, glared at him. "What are you doing back here anyway?" He swiveled his thick neck toward the DB5 and grunted. "Cool car."

Jordan grinned maliciously. "Bet Fatboy's pretending he's James Bond," he said. Behind him, a knot of students snickered.

Oz froze. Was it that obvious? Were his innermost secrets not so secret?

"That's a good one!" hooted Tank. "Who ever heard of a supersize superspy?"

"Double-O-LARD!" jeered Jordan, and the sharks and sharks-in-training clustered around him exploded with glee.

Shame rippled through Oz. Shame and humiliation. Tears started in his eyes, and he struggled to blink them back. He scanned the crowd, desperately searching for a friendly face. All he saw were sharks. And with the sound of their laughter ringing in his ears, he turned and fled.

CHAPTER 2

DAY ONE—
FRIDAY
1115 HOURS

At that very moment, a small nose—a very elegant little nose— emerged from an electrical conduit beneath a desk on the museum's fourth floor.

Elegant whiskers fanned out from either side of the nose. They twitched slightly, then waited. A full minute ticked by. The office was silent; the desk's occupant nowhere to be seen. The whiskers twitched again, and then the elegant little nose to which they were attached poked out further, followed by the nose's owner—a small brown mouse.

Quietly, she set down her mouse-sized skateboard. Expertly fashioned from a Popsicle stick and the wheels of a broken toy car, it was painted flamingo pink, thanks to the remains of a discarded bottle of nail polish. The mouse unstrapped her tiny safety helmet (a bottle-cap-and-rubber-band Forager's Special), hitched her small backpack (made from the thumb of a mitten) firmly into place, and shimmied up the phone cord.

She emerged on top of the desk a moment later. Keeping well out of sight, she skirted the telephone and clambered onto the stack of phone books propped beside it. She paused for a moment, then with a graceful leap propelled herself up through the air and onto the shelf above. She scurried into the shadows behind a dictionary and whispered into the microphone (part of an old cell phone headset) that was clipped to her glossy and impeccably groomed brown fur: "Agent in place."

"Check," replied a voice in her ear—a very elegant little ear. "Proceed with caution."

"Affirmative." The mouse inched forward. She peeked around the edge of the dictionary. Not a human in sight. "The coast is clear," she reported.

"Can you see the merchandise?"

She craned her neck for a better view of the desk below, scanning its surface with bright little eyes. There it was, inside a small plastic bag atop a red folder marked NEW ARRIVAL. Her whiskers twitched in excitement.

"Affirmative," she whispered. "I'll have it secured in two shakes of a cat's tail."

"Watch your back, now, Glory. Remember what happened last time."

The mouse named Glory grimaced. How could she forget? That little mishap earlier in the week had landed her on probation. Not something a field agent took lightly. Trust Fumble to remind her about it over the airwaves. She could practically hear the wisecracks zinging around right now down at Central Command.

It's not as if it was my fault, Glory thought sulkily, opening her backpack and drawing out a rubber band. *I was distracted.*

She scowled, recalling Tuesday afternoon's brush with disaster. Fumble had no business bringing it up. It wasn't as if she'd actually lost the Kiss of Death, after all. She knew as well as any mouse what would happen if that lethal weapon fell into the wrong paws. She'd managed to get it back in the end, and that was all that mattered. Besides, she'd like to see Fumble try to concentrate if he'd found the Black Paw in his mailbox right before an important mission.

Glory shivered. Even now, three days later, the thought of that menacing symbol sent a chill all the way to the tip of her tail. Marked for death, it meant. By none other than Roquefort Dupont, leader of Washington's rat underworld and the cruelest, most despicable rodent on the face of the planet. By dipping his mangy paw in ink and pressing it to a slip of paper, Dupont had announced to the world that she was on his hit list. Just as her father had been before her. And now, her father was gone—kidnapped and assassinated by Dupont and his conniving cronies.

Glory's bright little eyes glittered with tears at the thought of her father. He'd vanished three months ago, and she still missed him horribly. Time heals all wounds, everyone kept telling her, but she was beginning to think it wasn't true. Her father's death had left a hole in her heart that she doubted anything could ever fill.

Her whiskers quivering angrily, Glory shoved a safety pin through one end of the rubber band and jabbed it into the spine of the dictionary behind her. She'd show Fumble. No way was she going to let him get the best of her. Or Roquefort Dupont. Hit list or no hit list, she had a job to do.

Pushing all thoughts of her father and the Black Paw out of her mind, Glory tugged on the rubber band to make sure it was securely anchored, then tied a small loop in the other end and thrust a hind paw through it.

She crept to the edge of the shelf, steadied herself, and was just about to dive over the edge when— *BRNGGGGG!*—the phone on the desk below her rang.

Startled, Glory shot straight up into the air. She landed on top of a framed picture of a cat and glanced around in alarm, her heart pounding a rapid tattoo. Had she been spotted? No, still no humans in sight. But the telephone's insistent ringing always brought them running.

BRNGGGGG! Sure enough, Glory heard a door open and close just down the corridor. She didn't have much time. It was now or never. Glory slid down the back of the frame and scurried back to the edge of the shelf. She drew a deep breath—she had to concentrate! Much as she hated to admit it, Fumble was right. The Black Paw had rattled her. She'd been off her game these past few days, and she couldn't afford to make another mistake.

Willing herself to focus, Glory aimed for the desktop below and bungee-jumped headfirst toward the red folder, scooping the small plastic bag on top of it into her paws before the rubber band snapped her back up to the shelf again. It was a clean move, flawlessly executed, and so swift that even had a human been present, he or she might not have noticed at all. Moving quickly, Glory unhooked the rubber band and stuffed it into her backpack along with the merchandise, then ran for cover. She flung herself into a rose-patterned teacup on the far end of the shelf and huddled in its depths, panting. *BRNGGGGG!* Rapid footsteps announced the approach of the desk's occupant. Glory heard the clatter of the telephone receiver, followed by the murmur of conversation. She hoped fervently that her microphone wasn't picking up the frantic pattering of her heart. She could only imagine the mileage Fumble would get from that.

As if sensing her thoughts, her colleague asked, "Everything all right, Glory?"

Glory drew a deep breath, trying to calm herself. "Just swell."

"Did you retrieve the merchandise?"

"Affirmative."

There was a click as the telephone receiver was returned to its place, then the rustling of papers on the desk. A drawer opened and closed. Glory remained motionless, waiting for the human to leave. They always did.

Suddenly, her stomach lurched as the teacup in which she was hiding rose into the air. She ducked as something hit her on the head. "Ow!" She swatted the something aside and sat up, squinting at it. It was a square paper object with a string attached to one end. The string trailed over the edge of the cup. Glory gave a squeak of alarm. A teabag!

She sprang out of the cup and onto the saucer just as a stream of hot water came pouring in, but she wasn't fast enough. A few drops of steaming liquid spattered onto the tip of her tail. Glory squeaked again.

The human on the other end of the teakettle shrieked when she saw Glory and dropped both kettle and teacup onto the desk with a clatter. Glory leaped from the saucer just before it crashed. She ran, taking cover in the open tent of a birthday card.

"What's going on, Glory?" demanded Fumble.

Glory clutched her scalded tail and forced herself to breathe normally. A fine field agent she was. She'd never earn her Silver Skateboard at this rate. That had been a close call. Way too close for comfort. Still, no point in reporting that she'd almost become a mouse teabag. "Nothing," she said.

"Didn't sound like nothing," said Fumble suspiciously. "Sounded like a scream. A human scream."

"Stow it, Fumble. You're imagining things," snapped Glory. "I'm coming in. Over and out."

Glory peered out from inside the birthday card. The human was distracted, frantically trying to mop up the flood of hot water. Glory darted toward the back edge of the desk and catapulted off, catching the phone cord in one paw and rappelling neatly down to the floor. She landed with a light thump, jammed her safety helmet on her head, grabbed her skateboard, and wiggled into the conduit.

If Glory herself had designed Washington's International Spy Museum, she couldn't have created a more perfectly mouse-friendly work environment. The conduits that channeled all the electronic wires and cables for telephone, computer, audio, and video connections throughout the building not only allowed the Spy Mice Agency access to state-of-the-art equipment, but also doubled as a series of superhighways along which mice—especially field agents equipped with skateboards—could travel quite comfortably.

Glory ollied up and over a line of computer cable, slapped down into the conduit tube, and rocketed toward headquarters. She had to get to Julius before Fumble did. If her colleague reported this second mishap to her boss, she could lose her job. Even though being spotted by a human during a mission wasn't technically a breach of the Mouse Code—certainly not as serious a breach as actually talking to one—still, it wasn't something Julius would take lightly.

But even the thought of losing her job paled in comparison to the Black Paw, thought Glory grimly. She could always find another job. The Black Paw could mean the end of everything.

And as she carved her way down toward Central Command, it seemed to Glory that the wheels of her skateboard clacked out the same ominous phrase over and over again: *Marked for death . . . marked for death . . . marked for death . . .*

CHAPTER 3

DAY ONE—
FRIDAY
1130 HOURS

Oz ran blindly, heedless of anything but his dire need to escape. Behind him, Jordan and Tank were rallying the sharks for the chase. The hunt for Delilah Bean had been abandoned; he, Oz, was proving far better sport.

"Don't let him get away!" hollered Jordan.

Huffing and puffing, Oz lumbered on through the exhibits. *Ninja. Cloak. Dagger. Shadow.* With its high-tech lighting and exposed pipes running along the ceiling, the museum looked like the inside of a submarine. Oz didn't stop to admire the view, however; nor did he linger by the display cases full of gadgets (*hollow coins for hiding messages! lock pick kits! video camera sunglasses!*), disguises, and tips on the spy trade. Oz had a tiny head start, and he wasn't about to waste it. There was no way he could outrun the sharks. He'd have to outwit them.

"There he goes!"

"Get him!"

Oz glanced frantically back over his shoulder. The sharks were gaining on him. For once, though, he held the advantage. For once, the odds weren't stacked overwhelmingly against him.

Oz's father was the manager of the museum's Spy City Café, and since moving from California to Washington, D.C., two months ago, Oz had spent nearly every afternoon here in the building at Ninth and F Streets. When the dismissal bell rang at Chester B. Arthur Elementary School, Oz hopped the bus from Georgetown to Dupont Circle, then transferred to the Metro's red line for the short subway ride to the museum. He knew its layout like the back of his hand.

He also knew he couldn't last much longer. Oz didn't even run this hard in P.E. Sweat was dripping off his forehead and spattering onto his glasses, which had slid down again and were perched on the end of his nose. He swiped at them and ducked into the Secret History of History exhibit.

A quiet room with red walls, polished wood floors, and oriental carpets, it was usually a soothing place. A place Oz liked to hang out and read all about espionage—

information he figured he'd need someday when he was a spy. It was here that he'd gotten the idea for his social studies report about the Trojan Horse, the trick the ancient Greeks used to infiltrate and conquer the city of Troy. Oz didn't linger now, though. Now the red paint on the walls seemed to flash "Warning!" and "Danger!" He fled past the model of the hollow wooden horse with Greek soldiers crawling from its belly and ran on.

Emerging into a hallway, Oz paused for a fraction of a second, panting heavily. To his left was Fly, Spy!—an exhibit about World War II surveillance pigeons. To his right was the Library, with famous books about spies lining its shelves. Both were dead ends. He stared at the long hallway ahead. If he kept running, he'd probably pass out. Then the sharks would have him for sure. There was no other option; he'd have to risk the wrath of museum security.

Oz darted to the left toward a floor-length red velvet curtain. A rope was draped across it, on which hung a No Admittance sign. Oz ignored the warning and ducked under the rope. He pushed past the curtain to the stairway beyond and paused, wheezing.

"Hey, where'd he go?" It was Tank. He was close—heart-stoppingly close. Just on the other side of the curtain, in fact. Oz held his breath.

"He can't have gone far," Jordan replied. "Did you see him run? He waddles like a possum."

"Yeah," said Tank, sniggering. "Maybe he hides like one too. He's probably stuffed under a table or something. I'll double back."

"We'll keep going," said Jordan. "Send someone for me if you find him."

Oz heard the sharks walk away. His heart started beating again. His ruse had worked!

"Hey, what's behind that curtain?"

It was Tank again. Oz froze. He squeezed his eyes tightly shut, hoping that for once, just this once, maybe he really would turn invisible. And then—

"You boys move along now," said another voice. A gruff voice that Oz recognized. It was Herbie, one of the security guards. "You see the sign. That's off limits. Nothing for you to see back there."

Tank grunted, and Oz heard him shuffle reluctantly away.

"Never mind, guys," said Jordan to the rest of his followers. "We'll find him. He can't have gone far." And with that, he too moved off.

Oz rested where he was for a few moments, breathing shakily. His luck had held. He'd bought himself a little time. The sharks would catch him eventually—they always did—but for now he was safe.

Oz tiptoed up the stairs to the fourth floor, where a warren of cubicles housed the museum's administrative offices. He crept quietly past them to the elevator and emerged moments later on the ground floor. Passing under the statue of Feliks Dzerzhinsky, the former head of Russia's dreaded secret police, which hung suspended from the lobby ceiling, Oz took shelter in the hallway behind the Spy City Café. There he crawled under an open metal stairway and wedged himself into the shadows. The smell of chocolate chip cookies wafted out from the kitchen. He sniffed the air longingly. Chocolate chip cookies were his favorite, and his dad had promised to bake a fresh batch as a treat for him and his schoolmates. But going into the café meant he'd have to talk to his dad, and Oz wasn't ready to face his dad just yet. His dad could read him like a book. One look at his hot, sweaty, tear-tracked face and his dad would know that he, Oz, had failed yet again. That his son was a fat loser with no friends.

Starting over at a new school was never easy, especially for a chubby kid with a weird name. Oz knew this from bitter experience. He'd done it four times already since kindergarten, thanks to his mother's career as an opera singer. Seattle, San Francisco, Atlanta, New York—

all had been home at one time or another in the past few years. And now they'd landed here in Washington, D.C., where his mom would start her new job at the National Opera as soon as she returned from her Australian tour.

Oz slumped further into the shadows. He'd hoped maybe this time things would be different. Maybe this time he'd fit in. Make some friends. He'd even managed to make a bit of a game of things by pretending that staying off the radar screen was training for his future career as a spy. At his last school, Oz had managed to keep away from the sharks—and there were sharks at every school, he'd learned—until nearly Valentine's Day. But here it was only Halloween and he was already shark bait.

Oz hung his head. Some secret agent he'd make. He was a complete failure as an aspiring spy and as a human being. He didn't have one single friend. Not even Delilah Bean, the sharks' other favorite target. *Why did I even bother trying to protect her?* Oz thought glumly. It wasn't as if she'd spoken two words to him since the beginning of school.

"Loser," he whispered to himself, and slumping farther into the shadows, he surrendered to his dark thoughts.

Just then, at the far end of the hallway near the Ninth Street entrance, an elegant little nose emerged from a ventilation shaft. The nose caught the scent of chocolate chip cookies and twitched appreciatively. A second later Glory poked the rest of herself through the hole. Frowning, she plunked her flamingo pink skateboard onto the hallway floor and placed one hind paw atop it. With the other, she gave a powerful thrust and sped toward the stairway. So consumed was Glory with worry about the Black Paw, and her father's death, and whether Fumble had tattled to Julius, that she didn't see Oz sitting motionless beneath it.

Nor did Oz, still mired in misery, notice Glory.

Her face set in a scowl, whiskers sticking out like angry quills, Glory ripped down the hallway at a tremendous speed. At the last minute, she spotted Oz's tennis shoe. She squeaked in alarm and tried to swerve out of the way, but it was too late.

"EEEEEEEEEYOWWWWWWWW!" she cried as she collided with Oz's foot. Glory's skateboard went flying in one direction; she went flying in another.

The skateboard landed with a crash and so did Glory. She lay flat on her back for a long moment, stunned and breathless. *What the heck was that?* she wondered. Her helmet had been knocked askew and she couldn't see a thing. She reached up with one paw to push it aside and assess the damage, and as she did so she gave another frightened squeak. Oz was on his knees beside her, his face looming close to hers.

Boy and mouse stared at each other in shock.

Glory gaped at Oz, frozen with fear. Her bright little eyes flicked toward the narrow gap under the Ninth Street exit door. Could she make it? Her whiskers quivered in terror and her heart was pounding so hard she was sure the human could hear it. Every instinct in her little mouse body told her to run. But as she stared up at Oz, she felt an odd prickling of recognition. There was something familiar about him, something she couldn't quite put her paw on.

He didn't look familiar at all—just a round human boy with a round moon of a face topped with a shock of pale blond hair. Round wire-rimmed glasses partially obscured his eyes. A shame, thought Glory, for the boy's eyes were his best feature. Dark as bittersweet chocolate, they shone with an alert intelligence that— Glory gasped. It was the eyes! The boy's eyes were familiar!

She cocked her head and scrutinized Oz carefully. He knelt in the shadows, motionless, inspecting her just as carefully. And then in a flash Glory had it. The boy reminded her of her brother B-Nut!

Glory smacked a paw against the side of her head and shook herself vigorously. The crash must have knocked more than the wind out of her. As bright as B-Nut? Impossible. The boy was only human, after all.

"Are you hurt, little mousie?" whispered Oz fearfully. The mouse had hardly moved since the crash. He desperately wanted to pick her up and inspect her for injuries, but he was afraid she might bite him. Not that she looked dangerous. She looked—she looked—well, to be honest, she didn't look like any mouse Oz had ever seen before. That thing on her head could almost be a helmet. And the Popsicle stick—if he wasn't entirely mistaken, she had been riding it like a skateboard.

"Just a little road rash," Glory responded automatically, the words popping out before she could stop them.

She gasped. So did Oz, who scrambled hastily backward in panic. Glory's bright little eyes widened in fear. Her paw flew to her mouth. She'd just spoken to a human! She'd broken the Mouse Code!

Oz stared at her in disbelief. "You—you can talk?" he stuttered, prodding anxiously at his glasses. He must be hallucinating.

Glory stared back at him in alarm, her paw still firmly clamped over her mouth. If Julius got wind of this, she was finished. Boy and mouse regarded each other warily. For the first time, Glory noticed that the boy's cheeks were tracked with tears. She felt a rush of sympathy. He looked as miserable as she felt.

Hoping she wouldn't regret this later, Glory nodded slowly. She sat up and took her paw away from her mouth. "Tough morning?" she asked.

Oz gaped at her stupidly, at a loss for words. Finally, he shrugged, but made no move to come closer.

"Me too," said Glory.

They eyed each other again. Oz's gaze fell on the flamingo pink skateboard, and he flicked it toward her with a pudgy finger.

"Thanks," said Glory. She stood up and brushed the dust off her glossy brown fur. Then she thrust out a paw. "I'm Glory Goldenleaf, by the way."

Oz hesitated. He was still convinced that this was all a dream. A very bizarre dream. Or if it wasn't a dream, maybe it was a trick. What if the mouse—what if Glory—bit him? Those tiny teeth looked needle sharp.

"It's okay, I don't bite," said Glory, accurately reading his thoughts.

Oz blushed. He scooted closer, still a bit reluctantly, and reached out a tentative forefinger. "Oz Levinson," he managed to croak, and they shook solemnly. "That was some wipeout."

"Crash and burn is my specialty," Glory said ruefully.

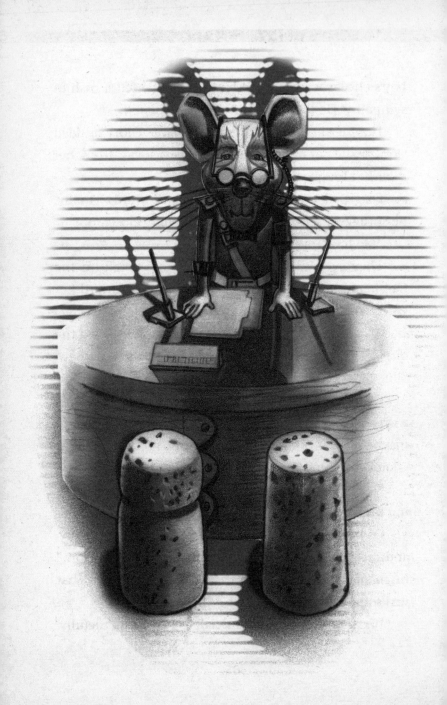

"If there's lame air, I'll find it. So is that Oz as in the movie?"

Oz cleared his throat. "Uh, no," he said. "Not exactly."

"Then Oz as in what?"

"Uh, Oz as in . . . as in . . ." Oz's voice dropped to a whisper. "Oz as in Ozymandias."

Glory's whiskers twitched. "You mean the poem 'Ozymandias'?" she cried in delight. "*'I met a traveller from an antique land'*—that poem?"

Oz nodded glumly.

"I love Shelley!" said Glory. "He's one of my favorite poets!"

Oz gaped at her again. "He is?"

"Sure, I've read all his poems."

Oz's mouth dropped open even further. "You mean, you can read?"

Glory shrugged. "Sure, can't you?"

"Well, of course," replied Oz, flustered. "All fifth-graders can read."

"So can all mice," said Glory.

Oz wanted to pinch himself. He was talking to a mouse. A mouse who could read. A mouse who rode a skateboard. And more than that, a mouse who was friendly. Who hadn't made fun of his name.

"I hate my name," Oz blurted.

Glory seemed astounded at this news. "Why?"

"It's stupid, and everyone makes fun of it when they find out." Which they always did. The sharks had a nose for stuff like that. And even though he always wrote just "Oz" on his school forms and assignments, somehow the teachers always found out, and then they had to read the stupid poem aloud, and then that was that. He wasn't invisible anymore. He was on the radar screen. Shark bait. With a name like Ozymandias, he might as well have a bull's-eye painted on his forehead.

"Yeah, I guess I know a little something about that," said Glory.

"Really?"

Glory nodded. "Uh-huh. My real name is Morning Glory."

"Morning Glory, like the muffin?" said Oz.

"You got it."

"What's wrong with that?"

Now it was Glory's turn to be embarrassed. "Oh, nothing, I guess. My mother is from the Bakery Guild. It's a family tradition. A stupid one. She named all of us mouselings after sweets. I'm part of the muffin litter— 'batch,' as she puts it. So are my sisters Pumpkin and Blueberry, and my brothers Bran, Chip—that's short for Chocolate Chip—and B-Nut. For Banana Nut."

Oz's forehead furrowed as he considered this information. "Makes sense," he said, nodding slowly. "But I still don't see why that's embarrassing."

Glory stroked the tip of her scalded tail, reluctant to admit the truth. If it wasn't for her name, no one would ever guess that she was half house mouse like her mother. In looks, thankfully, she took entirely after her father, the dashing field mouse general Dumbarton Goldenleaf, commander-in-chief of D.C.'s illustrious Mouse Guard. Before Dupont sent him the Black Paw, that was, Glory thought sadly.

She jerked her head up. Dupont! The crash had driven all thoughts of the rat's hit list—and her mission—out of her mind.

"I've got to go," Glory said hastily, gathering up her things and hopping back onto her skateboard. "I'm late."

"So soon?" said Oz, disappointed. Glory was the closest thing to a friend that he'd found since moving to Washington. The closest thing to a friend since kindergarten in Seattle, in fact.

Glory heard the dejection in the boy's voice. She hesitated a moment, torn. She'd broken the Mouse Code! If she was lucky, no one had spotted her. She might be able to get away with it this once. But if she encouraged further contact, she was risking her career.

Oz regarded her solemnly, his brown eyes—so like B-Nut's—brimming with sorrow.

Glory sighed. "Tell you what, kid," she said. "Do you know what a dead drop is?"

Oz nodded. He'd learned all about dead drops— what spies called the places they left information for each other—up in the Top Secret exhibit.

Glory tapped the bottom rung of the stairs with her paw. "This will be our dead drop. If you ever want to reach me, just leave a note taped underneath."

Oz brightened. "Okay," he said. "I'm around here a lot after school. My dad runs the café."

"He does? Is he the one who makes those great chocolate chip cookies?"

Oz nodded.

Glory sniffed the air. "Mmmm-mmmmm. Maybe you could leave me one later."

"Sure," promised Oz.

Glory waved a paw. "Good luck, Oz."

"Good luck, Glory."

And with that, Glory leaped onto her skateboard and zoomed off through a mouse hole in the shadows.

CHAPTER 4

DAY ONE—
FRIDAY
1145 HOURS

"Morning, Glory!"

Glory rolled her eyes at the stout gray mouse offering a mock salute from across the Spy Mice Agency's Central Command.

"Stow it, Fumble," she snapped, adding "stupid house mouse," under her breath. What an idiot! If she'd heard that stupid greeting once, she'd heard it a million stupid times before.

"Julius wants to see you," Fumble added, a smug smile creeping across his broad face.

Great, thought Glory. *There goes my job.* She scowled at her colleague in reply, squared her elegant little shoulders, and strode across the room.

The Spy Mice Agency headquarters hummed with activity. In one corner, a cluster of mice—including

Fumble—were seated on empty film canisters around the overturned margarine tub that served as their conference table. Some were busy scribbling reports with pencil stubs; others were listening intently through mouse-sized headphones (made from pistachio shells and pipe cleaners) to radio transmissions from field agents still out on assignment. Including Glory's own brother B-Nut, who was on his daily aerial surveillance run.

Thinking of B-Nut softened Glory's scowl. She glanced over at the opposite corner of the room where her other brother Chip and his fellow Foragers were busy unloading their bulging backpacks.

"Good haul today, Chip?" she called.

Her brother grinned and held up a belt buckle, a toy whistle, a handful of paper clips, and a pacifier. "Prime stuff," he replied. "Can't wait to see what the lab whips up out of these."

In yet another corner, the computer gymnasts were limbering up for their shift, which would begin upstairs on the administrative floor after the museum closed. While some performed a series of yoga stretches, others leaped up and down in formation as the lead mouse called out, "QWERT! ASDF! YUIOP!"

There but for a bit of luck go I, thought Glory. Just last summer she'd been plucked from those very ranks to train as a field agent. Glory had always been a good speller in school, and joining the computer gymnasts— mice trained to use human keyboards after hours to tap out e-mail messages, surf the Internet, and so on—had seemed a natural career step. She could have gone far with those skills, for good computer gymnasts were needed everywhere here in the nation's capital. Still, Glory was grateful that she had caught the eye of the Spy Mice Agency director, who had recruited her as a field agent instead.

As for herself, Glory had one goal and one goal only—to earn her Silver Skateboard. The highest honor that could be bestowed on a Spy Mice Agency field agent, the Silver Skateboard was her passport to adventure. Only the elite Silver Skateboard agents got the glamorous European postings—London, Paris, Berlin, Rome. Earning a Silver Skateboard was her ticket to the world. If she could keep out of trouble meanwhile, that was.

Behind her, the whispering started again. It had become nearly constant in the wake of Tuesday's fiasco, when Glory had been ambushed on her way back from a retrieval mission by Gnaw, a sly one-eared rat who was one of Dupont's top aides. Though hardly the brightest candle on the birthday cake, Gnaw had put up quite a fight, and Glory had almost lost the priceless Kiss of Death in the scuffle. Almost.

Let them talk, thought Glory furiously, looking back over her shoulder. Across the room, Fumble winked and waved.

"Stupid house mouse," she muttered again, not as quietly this time.

Glory slung her backpack onto a sardine can desk with an angry thump. Behind the desk sat an elderly mouse. His steely gray fur was mottled with age, and his eyes, once round and bright as little black beads, were now dim, but Julius Folger had the dignified bearing of an elder statesmouse. If Julius's other faculties were dulled with age, however, his hearing was still exceptionally keen, and he chided Glory softly as he reached for her backpack.

"I heard what you said to Fumble," he told her. "I do so hate that sort of thing amongst my team members. There's no shame in being a house mouse, my dear, and you must learn to stop using it as an insult. Don't forget that I too am a house mouse."

"Of the Library Guild, Julius!" Glory protested. "The Folger Shakespeare Library mice are one of our city's most honorable families, and that hardly qualifies you as an ordinary house mouse."

The Spy Mice Agency director regarded her shrewdly. "Avoid the ordinary at all costs, is that it?" He sighed. "*Mus musculus.* Ordinary house mouse. Well, who's to say what's ordinary and what's not? Fumble is a good worker—dependable, thorough, and mostly honest."

"Desk job," said Glory scornfully.

Julius peered closely at Glory, whose expression was mutinous, then replied tartly, "Need I remind you of your own house mouse heritage?"

"Only half," muttered Glory.

"And a fine half it is," said Julius. "I know your mother, Gingersnap, as well as I knew your father, and you have inherited many fine traits from both of them. Never be ashamed of who you are, Glory."

Glory sniffed, unconvinced.

Julius sighed. "So much of my wisdom is lost on you youngsters."

Unzipping her backpack, he reached inside. A crowd of curious mice quickly gathered, jostling Glory as they vied for a clearer view.

"Hey, watch it!" she said sharply as Fumble stepped on her tail.

"So sorry," said her pear-shaped colleague. "An accident."

Glory eyed Fumble with suspicion. *Accident my paw,* she thought, but not wanting to risk further scolding from Julius, she held her tongue.

"Well done, Glory," said Julius, drawing out the backpack's contents and laying it on the desk in front of him. "Well done indeed."

The elder mouse's praise melted over Glory's wounded spirits like glaze on a warm cinnamon roll. She perked up. Maybe she wasn't in trouble after all. The thought of cinnamon rolls made Glory's stomach rumble. It was lunchtime, and she was hungry. The scent of freshly baked chocolate chip cookies wafted down from the café overhead, reminding her of Oz. She hoped he would remember to leave her one.

Glory leaned in closer for a better look at the object on Julius's desk. It was nearly as big as Fumble's fat head and appeared to be a wristwatch. Glory regarded it with as much interest as the others, for although they all knew the object's true function, only Julius—who had read both the inventory report and the operating manual—knew for certain how to operate it.

The elderly mouse turned the watch over and released a small metal catch with his paw. The back sprang open, revealing a nest of mechanical parts, along with a tiny lens.

"Ahhhhh," breathed the gathered mice.

"Very nice," agreed Julius, poking at it delicately. The object was not a wristwatch at all, but a miniature camera. A human spy camera.

"Steineck, German-made, circa 1949. Just as described." He picked it up in his paws and looked through the lens at his gathered colleagues. "Where's Bunsen?"

The crowd parted and a slim white mouse stepped forward. He glanced quickly at Glory and reddened ever so slightly, a very faint blush that darkened only the tip of his tail and the tip of his nose. A blush so barely perceptible it would have gone unnoticed but for the fact that Julius happened to swing the camera around just then. He zoomed in on Bunsen's nose.

"You wanted me, sir?" said Bunsen, his question ending in a nervous squeak.

Julius lowered the camera and gazed at the nose in question. A slightly-more-pink-than-usual nose. "Take this to the lab and get started," he ordered, passing the camera to Bunsen. "You have my authority to use the full resources of the Foragers' Cupboard. There's no time to be lost—the replica must be back upstairs before the humans arrive at work tomorrow morning."

"Yes, sir," said Bunsen dutifully. With a last glance

at Glory, he sped off toward the lab with the watch-camera.

Julius stroked his whiskers thoughtfully. He wondered if Glory was aware of the fact that Bunsen admired her. Not that he didn't understand the appeal—Morning Glory Goldenleaf was a most attractive creature, after all, and since the beginning of time there had always been something particularly alluring about spies. Case in point: their own Mata Furry. A genuine mouse fatale, she had certainly never lacked for suitors. This held true for spies in the human world as well, he had heard. What was that fellow's name in those excellent espionage novels he'd read long ago in his youth? Agent Double-O-Something, the one who always got the girl. Band? Bund?

But still, a lab mouse and a field mouse? Julius shook his head. It would never work. They were just too different. Bunsen, with his steadfast, cautious nature and keen, probing mind, was the perfect scientist. And Glory, with her field mouse heritage of bravery, cunning, and slightly rebellious attitude, had all the makings of a superb secret agent.

Julius shrugged philosophically. Bunsen was a smart one; he'd see soon enough which way the wind was blowing. There was no need for Julius to go sticking his elderly and decidedly unromantic whiskers in where they didn't belong.

"The rest of you get back to work as well," he said, dismissing the crowd of curious onlookers.

As the mice began to disperse, Glory gathered up her backpack and skateboard and started to walk away.

"Not you, Glory," said Julius. "You stay."

Glory's spirits drooped again. *Here it comes,* she thought. *Good-bye, Silver Skateboard. Au revoir, Paris and Rome.* She turned and faced her boss, bracing herself for the worst.

"I hear you ran into trouble on this mission," said Julius.

Glory whisked her tail behind her, hoping her boss hadn't noticed its scalded tip. "Trouble?" she replied innocently.

"Fumble believes you were spotted by a human."

She knew it! The little weasel *had* tattled! Glory shot Fumble, who was watching the exchange with avid interest from across the room, a skewering look. He smirked and saluted again. Fuming inwardly, Glory turned back to Julius. "Well, maybe not exactly spotted," she said.

"Not exactly? Enlighten me." Julius crossed his paws on his chest and waited.

"I, uh, well, I suppose there may be a *slight* possibility

that I was seen, but only a slight one," said Glory. "The human was distracted." By a mouse teabag, she refrained from adding.

"I see," said Julius. He shook his head sadly. "Glory, Glory, Glory. I just don't know what to do with you. Two close calls in one week! I know you're still grieving for your father, and it's understandable what with the Black Paw—"

Glory started to protest, but Julius held up a paw and silenced her. "It's understandable," he continued. "Not an easy thing to put out of one's mind. Perhaps a furlough is what you need."

A furlough! Glory gaped at her boss in dismay. A furlough was a forced vacation reserved for field mice who cracked under pressure. A furlough was practically the loony bin. A furlough was a tail's length away from being fired.

"Julius, please, not a furlough! I promise it won't happen again," she pleaded.

The elder mouse eyed her for a long moment. "Lucky for you the human didn't put in a call to the Exterminator," he continued. "We've been monitoring the phone lines ever since you were spotted."

The Exterminator! Glory's whiskers quivered at the thought. A visit from the Exterminator was just about the worst fate a mouse could face. If something she did were to bring the Exterminator to the Spy Museum—well, it would be straight back to the computer gymnast typing pool for her. If she was that lucky.

"Against my better judgment I'm going to give you another chance, Glory," said Julius. "An opportunity to redeem yourself. As my most promising new field agent—and the daughter of one of my oldest and most trusted friends, may he rest in peace—I feel I owe it to you. But I must warn you, three strikes and you're out."

Glory's spirits soared. She was being given another chance! She nodded vigorously. "I understand, sir. You can count on me, sir."

Julius sighed. "I hope so, my dear." He reached under his desk and pulled out a shiny metal cylinder.

"The Kiss of Death!" exclaimed Glory.

"Yes," Julius replied, rolling it across the desk to her. "It's a routine courier mission, nothing fancy. My counterpart from MICE-6 is in town from London for a conference and I've promised him a closer look. Might prove useful—it seems the rats of the European Union are growing restless as well."

Glory nodded. She'd seen the headlines. Britain, France, Germany, Spain—Dupont had been busy of late, stirring up unrest around the globe.

"Forewarned is forearmed," Julius continued. "And it seems only fair that we share our knowledge."

"Where do you want me to deliver it?" Glory asked.

"The British Embassy," Julius replied. "Sir Edmund Hazelnut-Cadbury will be expecting you at eighteen hundred hours on the nose. And Glory, straightforward as this mission may seem, we cannot ignore the significance of the Black Paw. I want you to take extra precautions. Keep a sharp lookout for Dupont's forces and don't let your guard down for a minute. They'll stop at nothing to hijack my best new agent—or the Kiss of Death."

And with that sober warning ringing in Glory's ears, Julius dismissed her.

CHAPTER 5

DAY ONE—
FRIDAY
1330 HOURS

"There you are, my little fortune cookie!"

Luigi Levinson swooped down on his son as Oz entered the café. To his horror, Oz saw that the restaurant's booths and tables were crammed with students from his school. At the sound of his father's booming voice, everyone stopped talking and looked up.

Jordan and Tank twirled around on their stools at the counter. Oz saw them exchange smirks. He cringed. If he'd ever imagined he might be able to stay off the radar screen at Chester B. Arthur Elementary School, that hope was now completely and utterly dashed. Luigi Levinson was not someone you could keep off a radar screen. A great bear of a man with a dark beard and mustache, Oz's dad was always calling him embarrassing things like "snickerdoodle" or "dumpling" or "sugar plum."

"I've made some treats for you and your little friends," his father boomed again, producing a tray of chocolate chip cookies with a flourish.

Oz saw Jordan mouth *Little friends?* to Tank and wished desperately that the floor beneath him would open and swallow him up.

Luigi Levinson waved the tray of cookies underneath Oz's nose. They were still warm from the oven, the chocolate chips all gooey just the way Oz liked them. But right now, the thought of food of any kind—even his beloved chocolate chip cookies—made Oz's stomach turn.

"Maybe later, Dad," he said faintly.

Oz's father moved away, bearing the tray toward the booths overlooking the National Portrait Gallery across F Street. Oz stood rooted to the spot, his face flaming with embarrassment.

Jordan and Tank slid down off their stools and swaggered over to him.

"My little *fortune cookie*?" sneered Jordan, careful to keep his voice low. Their teacher, Mrs. Busby, was seated just down the counter, deep in conversation with one of the parent chaperones.

Oz stared silently down at his feet. Over the years, he'd learned not to prolong the agony by taking the bait. The quicker he submitted to the humiliation, the quicker it would all be over. He just wished his dad didn't have to witness it.

Tank could hardly contain his glee. "Fattest fortune cookie I've ever seen!" he crowed, jabbing Oz in the belly. "Bet the fortune inside reads, 'Danger! Wide Load!'"

Some of the students seated nearby looked sorry for Oz, but most laughed right along with Jordan and Tank, relieved not to be shark bait themselves.

Oz glanced up and saw his father heading back in his direction. *Great,* he thought miserably. *Just in time to watch the sharks zero in for the kill.*

"Leave him alone."

The voice made Oz jump. He whirled around. Behind him stood his classmate Delilah Bean, skinny legs planted defiantly on the café floor, skinny arms akimbo. Tiny black braids exploded around her head like a dark halo, and the expression on her face was fierce.

"What's it to you, Dogbones?" scoffed Tank.

Before Delilah Bean could answer, Mrs. Busby looked up from her conversation and frowned. "Jordan, Sherman, are you two causing trouble?"

"Uh, no ma'am," replied Jordan meekly, casting Oz a venomous look.

"They were too," snapped Delilah Bean. "Just like they always do."

Mrs. Busby sighed. "Boys, I have had just about enough of you two today. Get back to your seats now, and stay there until we're ready to board the bus."

As Jordan and Tank scuffed reluctantly away, Oz turned to the brown-skinned girl beside him. They eyed each other warily.

"So how come you stuck up for me, Delilah?" Oz asked finally.

Delilah Bean scowled. "It's just D. B.," she said. "Nobody but my mother calls me Delilah."

Oz shrugged. "Okay. How come you stuck up for me, D. B.?"

"I dunno," his classmate said grudgingly, still scowling. "Maybe because you didn't rat me out upstairs to Jordan-the-Jerk and the other idiots."

Oz shifted uncomfortably. D. B. obviously didn't know how close he had come to doing just that. "Guess I owe you one," he mumbled.

"It was nothing."

They stood there awkwardly for a moment, and

then Oz's father materialized. "Ready for a cookie now?" he asked.

Oz grabbed one blindly off the tray. "Sure, Dad. Thanks."

"Thank you, Mr. Levinson," echoed D. B. politely, also taking one.

"Aren't you going to introduce me to your little friend?" Oz's father asked.

"Oh yeah, right," said Oz. "Dad, this is Delilah Bean—I mean D. B."

Luigi Levinson shook D. B.'s hand and regarded her with interest. "You must be Amelia Bean's daughter."

"You know my mom?" D. B. looked surprised.

"She was here at the museum with a camera crew last month," Oz's father replied. He turned to Oz and explained, "D. B.'s mother is a news anchor for Channel Twelve. We got to talking over lunch and found out that both of our little snickerdoodles were in the same class at school." He beamed at them. "I'm so glad that the two of you are friends. Oz, perhaps you'd like to have Delilah—I mean D. B.—stop by the museum with you someday after school."

"Whatever," mumbled Oz, his face flaming again. *Snickerdoodles!* He could only imagine what D. B. must be thinking.

His father wandered away again, and Oz stared down at his shoes. He wondered what James Bond would do in this situation. Oz took a bite of cookie. He frowned. Did James Bond even have a father?

"It's okay if you pretend not to know me," said D. B. gruffly. "Once we're around the others, I mean. I know your dad was just being nice about inviting me here after school and all. I won't mind if you don't."

Oz gave D. B. a sidelong glance. The fierce expression had returned to her face. She was lying, anyone could see that. She would too mind. So would he if he were in her shoes. Not that he wouldn't have said exactly the same thing. To protect himself. To slip under the radar once again.

Oz cleared his throat uneasily. First Glory, and now D. B. Not exactly friends, perhaps, but not sharks, either. Maybe his luck was finally starting to turn. "You can come here with me sometime," he managed to blurt out. "It would be fun. Maybe tomorrow even, since it's Saturday."

D. B.'s face softened, although she didn't actually smile. "Yeah," she said. "That'd be okay. I'll check with my mom."

Mrs. Busby stood up just then and made her way to the center of the café. "Listen up, students!" she shouted, clapping her hands to be heard above the din. She waited until the room grew quiet. "I have an announcement to make! First of all, let's give Mr. Levinson a round of applause for those delicious cookies."

Cookies! Oz glanced down at the half-eaten cookie in his hand in dismay. He'd almost forgotten. He'd promised to leave one for Glory. As the room erupted in cheers, he searched for the tray, finally spotting it on the counter nearby. Empty! Not a single crumb was left. Sorrowfully, Oz wrapped the remains of his cookie in a napkin, hoping Glory wouldn't mind that he'd taken a few bites. He'd leave her a little apology note along with it before he got on the bus.

"And now, students, I have another announcement to make. Thanks to Oz's father, the fifth and sixth graders at Chester B. Arthur Elementary have received a very special invitation."

Uh-oh, thought Oz, his stomach plummeting. What was his dad up to now?

"We have all been invited to attend the museum's annual Halloween 'Come as Your Favorite Spy' masquerade ball this Sunday night! Won't that be fun?"

The room erupted in cheers again. Oz stared at his teacher, aghast. Fun? He couldn't think of anything *less* fun! This was a catastrophe! He'd had his costume ready for weeks now. He'd been planning to go as James Bond. He'd found an old tuxedo at the thrift store and everything. But now—well, Oz could only imagine the agonies of embarrassment and excruciating torture that would await if he turned up as Agent 007 at a party with Jordan and Tank. His secret fantasy exposed to the sharks for ridicule.

As the students crowded out the door toward the buses, Jordan and Tank sidled over to them. "So, Dogbones and Fatboy, is it?" said Jordan.

Tank elbowed him in the ribs. "Sounds like the title to a bad movie."

The two of them cackled at this display of wit. "Bet I know who you're going to show up disguised as, Blubberbutt," said Jordan.

Oz stared at the floor again. His luck hadn't turned after all. In fact, his luck had just run out. Completely out.

The sharks moved in for the kill. As Oz stood there helplessly, Jordan and Tank shoved their faces close to his and sang out in unison: "DOUBLE-O-LARD!"

CHAPTER 6

DAY ONE—
FRIDAY
1630 HOURS

It was rush hour on the roof
of the Spy Museum.

A long line of mice trailed from
the heating and air conditioning
vents across the roof's flat surface to its edge, where the
commuter patrol sorted them briskly according to destination.

"Keep it moving! Keep it moving!" The mice shuffled obediently forward toward the incoming Pigeon Air taxis. "Left for points north; right for points south, straight ahead for Dupont Circle. Climb on up there, make it snappy!"

Glory strode directly to the front of the line, the late-afternoon sun glinting off the tip of the metal cylinder that protruded from her mitten-thumb backpack. The other mice in line jostled each other as she passed, and Glory caught the words "Kiss of Death" whispered over and over. She ignored them.

When she reached the edge of the roof, she took the white-gloved patrol attendant aside and murmured something into his ear. He shot her a sour look, but nodded reluctantly.

"Agency business," he barked at a protesting commuter, placing Glory at the head of the Dupont Circle line.

Glory watched as a pigeon arrived in a flap of feathers, then took off again toward Union Station bearing a small passenger on its back. It was an efficient transportation system, and one that served them well. It served the pigeons well too, for in exchange for ferrying Washington's mice population to all points of the compass, the birds received food, water, and such grooming essentials as beak cleaning, feather brushing, down fluffing, and claw polishing.

"Quit daydreaming and get a move on! Your taxi's here!" The white-gloved commuter patrol attendant gave Glory a not-too-gentle shove. Before she could climb aboard the waiting pigeon, however, she was nearly trampled by Fumble.

"Sorry!" he called, sounding far too cheerful to be sorry at all. The pigeon grunted as Fumble heaved his

bulk onto its back. "Gotta fly—I'm late for a cheese tasting at the French Embassy!"

Glory glared at her colleague. Despite the fact that their activities at the Spy Mice Agency were supposed to be secret, Fumble was forever bragging about his work. He'd managed to make his humble duties sound so glamorous that he had quickly earned a spot for himself on Washington mouse society's A-list, and he spent his free time making the rounds of the city's most exclusive parties.

If only they knew that Fumble sat behind a desk all day, Glory thought crossly. Her colleague never budged off his plump bottom to do anything remotely dashing or dangerous. There'd be no cheese and hoopla for Fumble if the truth were known.

"If you get any bigger, you'll have to take the bus," she muttered.

"I heard that!" Fumble shot back, thrusting his feet into the stirrups (made of foraged paper clips) and giving the reins (foraged shoelaces) an angry flap. The pigeon onto which he had planted himself squawked in protest, then waddled resentfully into takeoff position. With a mighty grunt, it managed—just barely—to rise into the air. Fumble smiled spitefully down at Glory and blew her a kiss.

Glory heard snickers behind her, and she reddened. Obviously, Fumble was not about to let her forget Tuesday afternoon's blunder. Was the whole world talking about how she'd almost let the Kiss of Death slip through her paws?

Just then there was a flap of wings and whoosh of air very close overhead. The mice around her ducked and squealed, and Glory looked up to see her brother B-Nut, grinning as he waved to her from atop a barnstorming pigeon.

"Hey, no buzzing the commuters! You know the rules!" The patrol attendant ran after the low-flying pair, shaking his white-gloved paw angrily.

Glory grinned and waved back. A collective sigh went up from the female mice in line behind her at the sight of the handsome pilot. Her brother cut quite a dashing figure, and Glory watched as he and his pigeon landed with a graceful swoop in the surveillance corral. While B-Nut dismounted, two of the ground crew rushed forward and unhooked a small box that hung from the bird's neck. Glory knew it was not a box but a fly-spy cam, a camera containing the day's aerial surveillance film. Her brother's job was to keep a sharp lookout on the rats from the sky.

"Any sign of Dupont?" she called.

B-Nut, who bore a distinct resemblance to his sister—it was something in the set of the ears, and of course they both had the elegant Goldenleaf nose—shook his head. "Not so much as a whisker," he called back, crossing the roof toward her. "He's been keeping a low profile all week."

"Do you think he's up to something?" Glory asked.

Her brother shrugged. "Dunno," he said. "Julius thinks so. I guess we'll find out soon enough." He eyed the metal cylinder in her backpack. "Where are you going with that thing?"

"Courier job," Glory replied. All ears in line behind her were straining mightily in their direction, and she lowered her voice to a whisper. "British Embassy. Sir Edmund Hazelnut-Cadbury's in town, and MICE-6 wants a peek. Should be pretty straightforward. Which is a good thing. I can't afford any more mess-ups."

Glory told her brother about her close call earlier with the teakettle. She almost told him about breaking the Mouse Code too but in the end decided not to. She still wasn't sure what she was going to do about the note tucked in the bottom of her backpack. The one she'd found with the cookie at the dead drop, written on a napkin in a desperate scrawl. *Need your help. My life depends on it. Meet me here tomorrow at noon.* No, thought

Glory, until she was sure what she was going to do about Oz, it was best not to say anything.

"Maybe you should take Hank instead of Pigeon Air," suggested B-Nut. "Less margin for error that way. Some of these hacks should have been grounded years ago."

Glory glanced doubtfully at the wheezing specimen flapping its way toward her. "Maybe you're right. But isn't Hank ready to call it a day?" She looked across the roof to the corral where her brother's pigeon was getting his feathers groomed.

"Nah," said B-Nut. "Light duty today, what with no rats out on the streets." He spoke a few words into the microphone clipped to his fur and Hank nodded in response, then beckoned to Glory with his wing. B-Nut tossed her a quick salute. "Well, good luck, Sis. See you at home later tonight. Tell Mom not to wait dinner for me—the Acorns and I have to practice for Sunday night's gig."

"Okay," said Glory. The Steel Acorns were her brother's rock band. They'd been hired to play at the Spy Mice Agency's Halloween Eve gala two nights from now. Invitations had gone out weeks ago, and the city was abuzz with excitement. All of Washington's tail shakers would be there—Council members, representatives from the Embassy Guild, not to mention the stars of the Theater and Music Guilds, of course. And the top brass from the Mouse Guard.

With a flip of his tail, B-Nut sped off toward the vents that led down into the building. Glory heard more sighs behind her as her brother went by, followed by giggles. She rolled her eyes. Between his daytime job as a surveillance pilot and his after-hours job as lead singer for the Steel Acorns, B-Nut was very popular.

"You there! You're holding things up again with all your chitchat!"

"Sorry," said Glory to the patrol attendant. She stepped out of line. "Change of plans." As she headed for the surveillance corral, she heard a voice behind her.

"Miss Goldenleaf! Oh, Miss Goldenleaf!"

Glory turned to see Bunsen racing across the roof. He stopped in front of her, panting. The tip of his tail was bright pink.

"Yes?" said Glory.

"Uh, Miss Goldenleaf, we thought, uh, that is, *I* thought you might need, uh—here." He thrust a small object abruptly into her paws.

Glory inspected it curiously. It looked like a button on a chain. "What is it?"

The pink color crept up the entire length of

Bunsen's tail as he took the object from Glory's paws and placed it around her neck. "You wear it like this," he explained. "And see, the top unscrews, like this."

Glory glanced down. "It's a compass," she said in surprise.

Bunsen shook his head. "Not exactly. That was its original use, many years ago. One of your colleagues retrieved it just last week. In fact, the compass still works, but I've made a few, uh, modifications."

"So what does it do?" Glory eyed the small round object curiously.

"It's a homing device," the lab mouse continued. "I've outfitted it with a tiny transmitter." He glanced down shyly. "I—uh, I mean *we* can track you with it back down at Central Command. I heard about the Black Paw, you see, and I thought that, well, just in case . . ."

"In case Dupont nabs me, you'll know where to pick up the corpse?" Glory said.

Bunsen looked at her, appalled. "Oh no, Miss Goldenleaf! That wasn't my intention at all! It's so we can rescue you!"

Glory snorted. "Thanks, Bunsen, but haven't you heard? Dupont ships his victims home piece by piece."

Tears sprang to her eyes as Glory thought of the day

last summer when her mother had opened the door to discover a package on their doorstep. A package containing her father's tail.

"Oh, Miss Goldenleaf, I am most dreadfully sorry!" said Bunsen, wringing his paws in anguish. "I didn't mean to distress you!"

Glory shook her head. "Never mind. I know you didn't mean to." She glanced down at the homing device again and screwed the button top back on. "Thanks anyway, Bunsen. I appreciate the effort. You're true blue. And call me Glory, okay?"

The lab mouse's nose lit up like a bulb on a Christmas tree. He shot Glory an admiring glance. "You're very, uh, welcome, Miss, uh—Glory," he stammered.

"Ready?" It was Hank. Freshly watered, fed, and groomed, B-Nut's pigeon was resplendent in the late afternoon sun, his purple and gray feathers dust-free and gleaming.

"Later, Bunsen!" said Glory, climbing aboard.

Still blushing, Bunsen waved as Hank and Glory rose into the air above the Spy Museum. Glory waved back, then lifted her face to the sky and smiled, basking in the lingering golden warmth of late autumn. She loved to fly, especially this time of year, when the sticky heat of summer was gone.

Glory loved fall. She loved the crisp crunch of leaves beneath her paws at home in Dumbarton Oaks. She loved the smell of wood smoke drifting from Georgetown's many brick chimneys in the evenings. She especially loved the chilly autumn mornings, so perfect for burrowing down into the soft bits of flannel with which she lined her sleeping nook. Glory loved the bright blue of the sky, and the golds and russets with which nature dressed all of Washington's trees, and even the silly squirrels who hid their acorns and chestnuts and then forgot where they put them. This time of year brought a snap to everyone's step too. The tourist trade had dwindled to a trickle, and the city was all business once again—brisk with a sense of purpose as the humans got down to the work of running the country and the mice got down to the work of staying one step ahead of the rats.

"Your brother said you're heading to the British Embassy," said Hank. "When's your rendezvous?"

"Eighteen hundred hours," Glory replied.

"We've got a little time," said Hank. "How about taking the scenic route?"

"Sure."

Hank banked steeply, and Glory squeaked in delight as they swooped over the FBI building (the Feline Bureau of Investigation, where the G-mice kept a close watch on the city's bureaucats, including the fat cats on Capitol Hill). He turned and rocketed down Pennsylvania Avenue toward the Capitol, circling the building's majestic white dome, then flew east over the Supreme Court, home to the mice's Judicial Guild.

Now wheeling westward, the pair soared over the Smithsonian's National Air and Space Museum, then made a beeline toward the Washington Monument down the strip of green grass that formed the Mall. Glory gave another squeak as Hank swept in low on the final approach, then nudged his beak skyward at the very last minute and shot straight up, up, up—and then over the top of the lofty stone pillar to plummet down the other side.

Laughing and dizzy, Glory held on to the reins for dear life as they made a dash across the surface of the Reflecting Pool. Hank flew so low that she skimmed the water's surface with her tail, kicking up a narrow wake of foam behind them. To her right she could see the polished black wall of the Vietnam Veterans Memorial, while ahead lay the Lincoln Memorial.

Hank swooped inside and paused for a brief rest atop Honest Abe's marble head. It was cool and quiet inside the gleaming white structure, and Glory's voice echoed slightly in the stillness.

"I just love this city," she said dreamily.

"Yep," said Hank. "Me too. Wouldn't want to live anyplace else. Best way to keep your beak on the pulse of the nation."

"What's your favorite place in Washington, Hank?"

"Better to show than tell," the pigeon replied, and he spread his wings and took flight again, carving lazy loops southward in the air over the neighboring Tidal Basin. "Right here," he called back over his shoulder. "In the springtime, when the cherry trees are in bloom. No prettier place in the world. And I've seen a lot of the world. Didn't always roost in D.C., you know."

Glory looked down at the trees that rimmed the inlet, the lacy outlines of their branches visible through vibrant crowns of burnt-orange leaves. Come spring, the cherry trees would trade those bright, bittersweet halos for a cloud of pink blossoms that looked like cotton candy from the air. Glory closed her eyes. She twitched her elegant little nose, wishing for a moment that it were in fact spring so she could smell the sweet scent of cherry blossoms wafting skyward to greet them.

"Good choice, Hank," she said, opening her eyes again.

"How about your favorite spot, Glory?" the pigeon asked.

Glory didn't hesitate. "The Library of Congress."

Hank banked eastward. "Coming right up!"

Glory adored the Library of Congress, though she hadn't been able to bring herself to visit it since her father's death three months ago. It held too many memories. She and her brothers and sisters had spent such happy hours there with him as mouselings. Every week they'd made the long trip together from Dumbarton Oaks, and every week he'd read aloud to them from the books that lined the library's miles of shelves. Some of those humans could really write.

Glory missed more than the books and the memories. She also missed the marble floors, so perfect for after-hours skateboarding. It was along the library's broad hallways and down the smooth steps of the Great Hall, in fact, that she and her brothers and sisters had perfected their flip tricks and rail slides and grinds. And where she still spent much of her free time, practicing for the Silver Skateboard exam. Not lately, though. Not since her father's death. It was still too sad a place.

As Hank circled the library's rooftop, Glory shook off her melancholy thoughts. She looked down and felt a surge of pride. Generations of her mice ancestors had worked hard to make their civilization a success, all because they'd learned to read. It was a skill that the rats were too stupid or lazy to master, and one that had given the mice the edge in recent years. Because of the knowledge they had gained from books over the centuries, the Guilds had taken control of nearly all of the city aboveground, while the rats were consigned to Washington's sewers and subway tunnels and basements. And aside from the occasional territorial skirmish, the rats had remained reasonably content with the arrangement. They were partial to the dark anyway, and there was plenty of garbage below ground on which to feed. But that was before Dupont.

Roquefort Dupont wasn't Washington's average rat. Not by a long shot. Dupont wanted more. He wanted power. He wanted control. In short, he wanted everything. And what was worse, he hated mice with a passion. "The only good mouse is a dead mouse," was Dupont's motto, and in recent months, as he'd grown more restless and more determined to expand his territory (or "reclaim" it, as he put it, convinced that his ancestors had been swindled out of their rights), he and his army of rodents had struck out at the Guilds with vicious force. And now he wanted Glory Goldenleaf.

Glory shivered, troubled by thoughts of Roquefort Dupont and the dreaded Black Paw. Was her father's fate soon to be her own? Was his nightmarish end her destiny as well?

Hank finished his circuit of the library's rooftop. He dove toward Neptune's Court Fountain below, a spine-tingling descent that banished all thoughts of Dupont and doom from Glory's mind. She whooped with glee as the pigeon pulled up smartly and landed atop one of the stone turtles, deftly avoiding the spray of water that gushed from its silent mouth.

"You mice like to read, don't you?" Hank said.

"Yes, I suppose we do," Glory replied, glancing cautiously at the passersby. But the stream of briefcase-clutching humans who flowed past were intent on getting home, and no one seemed to notice the pigeon with the mouse on his back. Glory slipped off Hank and sat down beside him companionably.

"Never learned, myself," the bird said. "Don't quite understand what all the fuss is about."

Glory trailed her hind paws in the water. How could she answer that? She considered herself a mouse of action, but still, there was nothing she liked better than to curl up in a good book at the end of a long day. "Well, it's never too late to learn," she replied simply.

Hank bobbed his head and scratched at his breast

feathers with his beak. "Can't teach an old bird new tricks."

"Nonsense," said Glory. "A pigeon as clever as you could do anything he set his mind to."

Hank flapped his wings. "Kind of you, I'm sure. Maybe I'll give it a try someday." He cocked an eye at the fading sunlight. "Well, I suppose we'd best get a move on. Don't want you to be late for your rendezvous."

They were soon aloft again, and this time Hank didn't dawdle. He veered northwest toward Georgetown, flew over the White House and the National Geographic Society (home of the Explorers Guild), and shortly reached Dupont Circle. Glory gazed down at the traffic rotary with the park at its center. A handful of chess players sat at stone tables by the fountain in the fading light, intent on their games. She glanced over at the entrance to the Metro station. There, deep underground, Dupont had his headquarters. There, her father had met his end. The fur on the back of her neck prickled as she wondered if she too would meet her end in the subway station's shadowy depths. Best not to think about that right now, she told herself sternly. But as Hank flapped onward, Glory couldn't resist one last look.

"Wait, Hank!" she called.

The pigeon looked back over his wing at her. "What is it?"

"Could you circle around again? I thought I saw something."

"Sure." Hank tilted his wings slightly and doubled back.

"There!" shouted Glory. "By the subway entrance! It's Dupont!"

"I see him," said Hank. "No mistaking that ugly mug. Wonder where he's been hiding all week."

Dupont had spotted the two of them as well. He bared his sharp yellow teeth at them in an evil grin, and Glory shivered again, grateful that she was safely out of paw's reach atop Hank.

"That no-good rat is up to something," said Hank. "I can smell it."

"Maybe we should take a closer look," Glory replied. "While there's still daylight. Can you get us in lower?"

In response, Hank swooped toward the ground. As Glory leaned forward for a better view, the top of her backpack flapped open. The metal cylinder inside gave a lurch. Glory felt it sliding forward. She grabbed for it in alarm, but it slipped between her paws and went hurtling down, down, down through the air.

"The Kiss of Death!" cried Glory. "Oh, Hank, I dropped the Kiss of Death!"

"Hang on," said Hank, and folding his wings closed, he tucked his beak into his gleaming purple breast feathers and took a nosedive straight toward Dupont.

The metal cylinder flashed in the last rays of October sun as it spiraled toward the ground. The rat spotted it and raced forward, his paws stretched out greedily as he maneuvered to position himself beneath it. Glory tucked her hind paws through the paper clip stirrups and stretched out into midair as she too reached for the Kiss of Death.

In a flurry of feathers and fur, rat, mouse, and pigeon collided. Glory grabbed not the Kiss of Death but a pawful of Dupont's mangy hide instead. Dupont grabbed Hank, and the Kiss of Death went clattering to the ground and rolled away.

Hank let out a screech and pulled up sharply, leaving Dupont clutching a few purple feathers.

"Try again, Hank!" Glory urged, shaking Dupont's nasty gray hairs off her paw and grabbing the reins as they circled back. But it was too late. With a shriek of triumph, Dupont snatched up the metal cylinder and waved it at them like a trophy.

"Oh, no!" wailed Glory.

"It ain't over yet," replied Hank, and dive-bombed the rat once again.

Dupont was ready for them this time. As Glory reached for—and got her right paw around—the Kiss of Death, the rat grabbed her by the neck. The jolt nearly grounded Hank, who flapped his wings furiously trying to stay aloft. Dupont thrust his patchy face up to Glory's and fixed her with a fiery red eye.

"A Goldenleaf, if I'm not mistaken," he said. His raspy voice sounded like a bucket of nails tumbling down a garbage disposal. "I'd know those ears anywhere. Have a pair of 'em nailed to the wall down at HQ."

Glory paled. Dupont was talking about her father. "You're scum," she croaked, struggling to free herself. "Nothing but rat scum. Always have been, always will be."

Angered by her words, Dupont released the Kiss of Death and squeezed Glory's neck with both paws.

"Scum, am I?" he snarled. His breath reeked, and Glory's eyes watered. "I'll have you know I'm the descendant of kings! My ancestors kept your kind as servants!" He squeezed harder, and stars swam before Glory's eyes. She gasped for air. "Did you get the little present I sent you?" Dupont said, taunting her. "Didn't think I'd have the pleasure of your company so soon. But no one outruns the Black Paw. Not even a Goldenleaf."

Struggling mightily, Glory managed to free one of her hind paws. She aimed a kick straight at the rat's ugly nose. Dupont screeched and clutched at his wounded snout. As he did so, one of his claws caught in the chain around Glory's neck. It wrenched free with a forceful jerk that brought Glory tumbling off Hank. She landed on the pavement with a thud. Ignoring the pain, she leaped to her paws and sprinted toward the Kiss of Death, but Dupont was too quick for her. With a sinister grin, he snatched up the metal cylinder.

"The only good mouse is a dead mouse," he sneered, and lunged at her.

"Look out, Glory!" squawked Hank as the rat's sharp claws raked her shoulder. Swooping in, the pigeon plucked her from the pavement and they soared upward, Glory clutching at her rescuer's feathers for dear life.

"I'll make mousemeat out of you yet, mark my words!" screamed Dupont, shaking his paw at them angrily.

"Are you okay?" Hank called anxiously to Glory.

She nodded, wincing. She climbed gingerly up onto Hank's back and inspected her shoulder. Dupont had drawn blood. It could have been worse, though, she thought with a shudder. Much worse. And they still weren't out of danger. Below them, the rat had slung the homing device around his neck and was hefting the Kiss of Death onto his shoulder. He scanned the sky, then pointed it straight at them.

"Look out, Hank!" Glory cried out in warning. "Duck!"

Not a moment too soon, the pigeon banked steeply left. A puff of smoke emerged from the mouth of the small metal cylinder, followed by sharp report. Something whistled past them.

"What in tarnation was that?" shouted Hank.

"I told you, it's the Kiss of Death."

"I thought it was a lipstick!"

"That's what you're supposed to think," said Glory. "It's a pistol. Single-shot, four point five millimeters. It's Russian-made, circa 1965. KGB issue."

"A pistol?" Hank faltered slightly, and Glory clutched at his feathers again to keep from toppling off. He gave a low whistle. "No wonder Julius's tail was in a twist. All we need in this city are armed rats!"

No kidding, thought Glory, her injured shoulder throbbing ferociously. No mouse would be safe if that happened. Especially not one marked with the Black Paw. Dupont's razorlike claws would pale in comparison to armed rats. Glory's heart clutched in fear at the thought of platoons of rat snipers stationed throughout Washington, their sights all trained on her. She wouldn't be safe anywhere! She shifted uneasily on Hank's back, fearful that she had just signed her own death warrant.

As she wedged her paws back into the stirrups, a cooing noise above caught her attention. Glory looked up. She gasped in dismay. High above them circled another pigeon. Around its neck was a small box. A fly-spy cam!

Glory's heart sank. Could her luck possibly get any worse? The evening surveillance team had just captured the whole fiasco on film. Glory buried her face in her paws. Her career was ruined, and Dupont had sworn to make mousemeat out of her. She was doomed.

CHAPTER 7

DAY ONE—
FRIDAY
2200 HOURS

The rotary at Dupont Circle hummed with late-night traffic, headlights fanning out like bright spokes around the silent, dark hub at its center. The stone benches at the stone tables were empty of chess players, and the surrounding streets were almost as empty. Only a handful of humans were still out, most of them heading for the entrance to the Metro station, where escalators would whisk them to the trains far below.

There, deep in the bowels of the subway station, stood a bench in a shadowy corner. Beneath it lay a drain hole covered by a loose-fitting grate. The grate concealed the entrance to a tunnel that wound its way down, down, down to a lair far below the subway tracks. In that dank, cramped space as smelly as the ripe blue cheese for which he was named, Roquefort Dupont, Lord of the Sewers and supreme leader of Washington, D.C.'s rat underworld, paced back and forth in a fury.

"Rat scum, am I?" he blustered, whipping his mangy tail through the air angrily. He could hear the excited squeaks and squeals of his underlings echoing along the lair's many side tunnels. They were still busy rejoicing over the capture of the Kiss of Death. Dupont himself was in no mood for celebration. He'd been in a rage for hours, ever since his run-in with Glory. "I'll show her rat scum. Blasted uppity Goldenleaf. Who does she think she is, speaking to me like that? Me! Roquefort Dupont! The descendant of kings!"

Gnaw and Scurvy, Dupont's two top aides, exchanged a glance. The boss was in one of his moods again.

A pair of young rats-in-waiting, Limburger Lulu and Limburger Louie, watched anxiously as Dupont, muttering angrily to himself, booted an empty yogurt container into the air. It landed on a heap of crumpled, grease-stained lunch bags. Piles of garbage—the remains of rat delicacies pilfered from the trash cans in the subway station above—lay strewn about everywhere. Apple cores and moldy crackers, half-eaten cookies, cartons of soured milk, leftover turkey sandwiches turning green around the edges, candy wrappers and juice boxes and gum scraped from the undersides of benches.

Dupont whirled around. Glory's button compass was slung around his neck, and it whirled along with him. "Who am I?" he snarled savagely.

"You are Roquefort Dupont!" chirped his rats-in-waiting.

"And what is my lineage?"

"You are the great-great-great-great-great-great-great-great-great-great—" Limburger Lulu and Limburger Louie paused to suck in a lungful of air, then rattled on, "great-great-great-great-grandson of Camembert Dupont!"

"That's right, and don't you forget it!" roared Dupont. "Gnaw did once, and look what happened to him!"

Gnaw, an unattractive creature with close-set eyes and scruffy gray fur, reached up and clutched anxiously at his sole remaining ear. He'd lost the other in a tussle with Dupont several years back, when he'd tried to rival him for leadership of the rat kingdom. He hadn't tried again.

"That's right," warned Dupont. "You'd better hang on to it. Never know when someone might sneak up on you and bite the other one off!"

Gnaw gulped. The Limburger twins' heads swiveled from him to their boss and back again. Their round red eyes were bright with fear.

Dupont began to pace again. "Why should we be stuffed away down here in the dark, while Glory Goldenleaf and her kind enjoy the best this city has to offer?" he growled.

"But, Boss," ventured Scurvy, a bone-thin rat with prominent yellow teeth and whiskers that drooped nearly to the floor. "Rats like the dark."

"That's beside the point!" Dupont thrust his sharp snout into his hapless aide's face. Scurvy quailed, his beady red eyes bulging in terror. "I'm the descendant of royalty! Camembert Dupont lived in a *castle*! He had mice for *servants*! We should be the ones ruling this city, not those miserable little small-paws!"

Dupont kicked viciously at a slice of spoiled cantaloupe. Lulu and Louie quailed too. Scurvy and Gnaw exchanged another glance. A glance that clearly said it was best to stay out of the boss's way when he got like this.

"You!" said Dupont, whirling around again and whipping his tail toward Gnaw.

Gnaw, who was still clutching his single, flea-bitten ear, swallowed nervously. "Yessir?"

"*I want that Goldenleaf brat!*" Dupont ordered. "That little spy is too clever by half. If it weren't for her and those other wretched spy mice, we'd have gained access to the museum's weapons weeks ago." He speared Gnaw with a glance. "Whatever it takes, bring her to me, or by the Black Paw itself, I swear your days are numbered too."

Gnaw shrank back in alarm. His boss bared his teeth in what passed for a smile. "That's right," Dupont murmured, his voice oozing encouragement. He advanced menacingly toward his aide. "Fear is good. So is terror. I like to see both in an underling. Keep it up, Gnaw."

Gnaw nodded rapidly, and Dupont retreated and began to pace again.

"I can't quite decide what to do with that snip of a mouse once I get my paws on her," he mused. "The possibilities are so delicious. Endless bondage as my personal slave? Or death by slow torture—piece by furry piece?" He whirled around. "What are you waiting for?" he screamed at his startled aide, who leaped straight up in the air in fright. "Bring her to me! And watch your back, you bonehead. She's a sly one, just like her father."

As Gnaw scuttled off to do his superior's bidding, Dupont frowned. "The nerve of her! Rat scum, indeed!" His fiery red gaze landed on Limburger Lulu and Limburger Louie. "I think we've waited long enough, don't you?"

Lulu and Louie nodded instantly in agreement. They always nodded in agreement. That was their job.

Dupont's beady eyes turned toward Scurvy, who began chewing anxiously on his scrawny tail. His long whiskers drooped even farther and his skinny nose wrinkled in distaste as Dupont drew close. The commander-in-chief's breath smelled of three-day-old peach yogurt and rancid ham. Disgusting, even for a rat. But how did you tell your boss he needed a breath mint? The answer was, you didn't. Not when your boss was Roquefort Dupont. Scurvy closed his eyes and tried not to breathe instead.

"Call the troops together," Dupont ordered, hefting the Kiss of Death onto his shoulder and sighting along its barrel. "With this in our possession, we've finally got the upper paw. I'm moving up the schedule for Operation P.E.S.T. Control. We go in two days from now, on Halloween."

Lulu and Louie gasped. Scurvy's eyes popped open. "Halloween?" he squeaked in protest. Halloween was every rat's favorite holiday. All that lovely candy! And all you had to do was slink around in the shadows and wait for the short humans to drop a piece. "Aw, but Boss—"

"You have a problem with that?" Dupont aimed the

Kiss of Death at his aide and squinted menacingly.

Scurvy gulped. He shook his head.

"Good," growled Dupont. "It's time we showed those puny small paws who's in charge here."

As Scurvy darted off to do his master's bidding, he tripped over his whiskers and went flying head over tail to land in a heap of orange peels. He picked himself up, looked back fearfully, then slunk away into the shadows.

Dupont watched him go. He shook his head in disgust. "Idiots," he snarled, snapping a moldy potato chip in two with his razorlike yellow teeth. "I'm surrounded by idiots!"

CHAPTER 8

DAY TWO—
SATURDAY
1145 HOURS

Oz glanced at his watch.
"Hurry up, D. B.," he said.

"In a minute, in a minute," his classmate replied.

They were in the Spy Museum gift shop. The two of them had spent the morning roaming the exhibits together, and then they'd sat in on a workshop on disguises. Two former Central Intelligence Agency experts had demonstrated how real spies used tools of the trade to change their identities, transforming a young woman in the audience into an elderly crone with the use of a gray wig, thick glasses, and makeup.

"Hey, Oz, look at this!" said D. B., holding up a soda can. She unscrewed the top to reveal a secret compartment.

"Yeah," said Oz. "I've got one of those at home. Pretty cool, huh?"

"I'm going to buy it," his classmate said, adding it to the pile of souvenirs she was clutching—invisible ink, dissolving paper, and a fingerprint kit.

Oz had picked out a black baseball cap with SPY emblazoned across the front of it and a new book about James Bond. The book alone cost two weeks' allowance. Even though Oz had a whole shelf of books at home about his favorite secret agent, he still felt it was worth it. An aspiring spy could never know too much about James Bond.

"Are you ready yet?" he asked, glancing at his watch again. It was almost noon.

"Not quite," answered D. B.

Oz trailed after her. "How about I meet you in the café in a few minutes? I have to use the restroom."

"Sure," D. B. replied vaguely, inspecting a CD of spy music.

Oz paid for his purchases and hurried across the lobby toward the café.

"There you are, my little pizza pie!" cried his father, spotting him. "I've saved a booth for you and Delilah and me. How do grilled cheese sandwiches sound for lunch?"

"Great, Dad," said Oz, his stomach rumbling in anticipation. "And don't forget, it's just D. B. She doesn't like Delilah."

"Of course," his father replied, smacking his forehead with the heel of his hand in mock dismay. "How could I forget?"

Oz slung his bag of purchases onto the seat of a booth marked RESERVED. His father eyed it curiously. "What did you buy?"

"Oh, just a hat. And a book."

"Let me guess—James Bond?" Luigi Levinson smiled fondly at his son.

Oz smiled back. His dad knew about his secret ambition. "Yeah."

"Let's see the hat on you."

Reluctantly, Oz pulled the baseball cap out of the bag and put it on. He glanced around at the crowded café, but no one was paying him the least bit of attention.

"Looking good," said his father, nodding in approval. "Maybe I should get one, too."

Oz glanced at his watch again. "I'll be back in a minute, Dad. I gotta make a pit stop."

In the hallway behind the café, Oz didn't turn left toward the restrooms but right toward the metal staircase.

He crouched down on his hands and knees and peered into the shadows. No sign of Glory. He peered at the dead drop under the bottom stair. No note either. He glanced at his watch again anxiously. Two minutes to go.

Oz sat down under the staircase and hugged his knees to his chest. He couldn't tell his dad about the Halloween party. His dad wouldn't understand. He'd get the James Bond part, but he wouldn't understand about the sharks. His mom might understand, but she was in Australia and what could she do about it? D. B. would definitely understand his fear of the sharks, but Oz wasn't ready to tell her about the whole James Bond thing. She'd probably think it was stupid. That left Glory. She was the only one Oz could think of who might be able to help him.

He looked at his watch again. Now all he had to do was wait.

CHAPTER 9

DAY TWO—
SATURDAY
1145 HOURS

Glory had been waiting all morning.

Central Command was in an uproar. News about the Kiss of Death's loss had leaked to the press, and reporters from all the major papers—*Mouse Daily*, *Mouse Post*, *Washington Whiskers*, and even *Tattletail*, the city's most notorious tabloid—were clamoring for an official comment. Julius had been in meetings since dawn, first with members of the Council, then with Sir Edmund Hazelnut-Cadbury ("Highly displeased," was all that the pair of tight-lipped computer gymnasts who'd been called in to take notes would say), and now with the top brass from the Mouse Guard.

Glory, meanwhile, slumped miserably on a spool by her boss's desk, awaiting her fate. A white bandage covered the shoulder that Dupont had clawed. Across the room, Fumble could hardly conceal his delight at her misfortune. Glory was sure that the whispered rumors flying around Central Command ("International scandal!" was the latest) were his doing as well.

"Let him gloat all he wants. He's just jealous," consoled B-Nut, who'd stopped by to lend moral support. "Did you know Fumble wanted to be a field agent?"

Glory looked at her brother in surprise.

"That's right," B-Nut continued. "I overheard him talking to Julius right before we started spy school last summer. Julius told him he doesn't have the build for it. A polite way of telling him he's a gutbucket. Then you come waltzing in, plucked from the lowly ranks of the computer gymnasts, no less. Your job is a hundred times more exciting than his, and Fumble resents it."

"I suppose that would explain why he's always on my tail," said Glory, eyeing her portly colleague with distaste. "But I still think he's a stupid house mouse backstabber."

The doors to Central Command flew open and Chip, B-Nut's twin, entered the room, fresh from a foraging run. He spotted his siblings and made a beeline for Julius's desk.

B-Nut slapped him a high-paw. "Good run this morning, Bro?"

Chip nodded, dumping his duffel bag—made from a foraged baby sock—onto the sardine can desk. Out tumbled a penny, a plastic fork, a deflated balloon, and two fresh pieces of chewing gum.

"So, Glory," he said as B-Nut admired the haul, "any word yet?"

Glory shook her head. "I've been cooling my tail all morning," she said.

"Don't worry, you'll come through just fine. You always do."

"I don't think so, Chip," Glory replied. "Not this time. But thanks anyway."

Her brother gave her a quick hug, gathered up his things, and headed for the Foragers' Cupboard. Glory watched him go. Like B-Nut, Chip was true blue. He was also well on his way to becoming a Master Forager. "Never met a junk pile he didn't love," her father had always said. But besides the basic magpie instinct that all born foragers came into the world with, Chip possessed the requisite sense of honor. Any mouse could steal something, but true foragers abided strictly by the Forager's Code: "One man's trash is another mouse's treasure"—never taking anything that belonged to another, not even a human, but foraging only those items that had been lost or thrown away instead.

The Forager's Code made Glory think of the Mouse Code. Had she been dishonorable by breaking it? She squirmed uncomfortably on her perch and glanced at the clock on the wall. She was supposed to meet Oz in ten minutes. Even if Julius was through with her by then, she still wasn't sure if she was going to go.

The door to the conference room opened and a dignified gray nose appeared. "Glory, you may come in," Julius announced solemnly.

Glory hopped off the spool, and B-Nut patted her shoulder in encouragement. "Good luck, Sis," he whispered. "I'm rooting for you."

"Thanks, B-Nut," said Glory, and with a withering glance at Fumble, she marched into the conference room with her whiskers held high.

"Take a seat, Glory." Julius waved a paw at one of the empty corks that surrounded the circular wooden cheese box conference table.

Obediently, Glory sat. A trio of high-ranking officers from the Mouse Guard—her father's former colleagues—regarded her solemnly. Glory swallowed. Her throat was tight with anxiety, and she desperately wished she had a thimble of water.

"Glory, there's no easy way to say this," Julius began, shaking his grizzled head sadly. "I'm afraid I warned you, my dear."

"Julius, it wasn't my fault," Glory protested. "Dupont goes missing for days and finally surfaces— what else could I do? I had to take a closer look! I figured you'd want to know what he was up to."

"You were sent on a simple mission," countered Julius. "A routine courier job. And instead you took a risk that ended in disaster. *Disaster,* Glory! Do you realize what this means? Dupont finally has his paws on a weapon. He may be illiterate, but he's not stupid. It won't be long before he figures out how to replicate it. Imagine, Glory, armed rats swarming the streets of Washington! It could alter the balance of power in this city—no, the world—forever."

The Mouse Guard officers all nodded in sober agreement.

"We're going to do our best to retrieve the Kiss of Death," Julius continued. "Sir Edmund Hazelnut-Cadbury wants to call in MICE-6, says they've had centuries' more experience dealing with the likes of Dupont than we have, but the Council and I have full faith in our own resources. I'm sending in a Silver Skateboard team. They'll join forces with a commando unit from the Mouse Guard. The mission is in the planning stages now and they'll be ready to go in twenty-four hours. But meanwhile, Glory, I'm afraid there's no room here in the Spy Mice Agency for a cowboy."

Glory sagged on her cork. A cowboy, as she well knew, was the name for a spy who took unauthorized risks, often endangering his or her fellow agents. She stared hard at the table, willing herself not to cry in front of her father's fellow soldiers.

"Three strikes, Glory," said Julius softly. "Remember?"

Glory nodded miserably. Losing her job hurt worse than she ever could have imagined.

"I'm afraid it's out of my paws, my dear," said Julius. "You're fired."

CHAPTER 10

DAY TWO—
SATURDAY
1205 HOURS

Oz glanced at his watch.
Glory was late. He looked over at
the mouse hole in the shadows. Not
so much as a whisker in sight.

She's not coming, he thought in despair. *Glory's not coming.*

He'd give it five more minutes. Any longer than that, and his dad and D. B. would come looking for him. Oz pushed at his glasses and frowned intently at the mouse hole, willing Glory to appear.

Two more minutes ticked by. Oz sat up a little straighter. Was that a movement in the shadows? He craned his head forward, holding his breath. And then an elegant little nose poked out of the mouse hole.

"Glory!" Oz whispered joyfully. She had come after all!

Morning Glory Goldenleaf hauled herself listlessly

through the mouse hole in the wall. Her whiskers and ears drooped with dejection.

Oz spotted the bandage on her shoulder. "Glory, you're hurt!" he exclaimed. "What happened?"

"I just got fired," said Glory, and started to cry.

Very gently, Oz reached out his hand and placed it on the floor, palm up, next to her. "I'm so sorry," he said.

Glory hesitated only a second, then flung herself onto Oz's palm. All the pent-up emotions of the past week came pouring out.

"It's all my fault!" she sobbed. "I should have gone straight to Embassy Row, just like Julius told me. He warned me to be on my guard, but I saw Dupont and I thought I should take a closer look and—"

"Dupont? Julius? Embassy Row?" said Oz, mystified.

Glory swiped at her tear-stained fur. "It started three months ago," she gulped. "Last July, Dupont—that's Roquefort Dupont, leader of the rats here in Washington— kidnapped my father and assassinated him."

Oz's brown eyes widened in consternation. "That's awful!" he said.

Glory nodded. "My mother still hasn't left the house. We all miss him terribly."

Oz nodded sympathetically. He knew all about

missing someone. His mother was in Australia—but at least she was still alive. Very gently, he raised his hand and placed it on his knee so that he was eye to eye with Glory.

"And then, last Tuesday, Dupont sent me the Black Paw."

"What's that?"

"A death warrant," Glory replied. "Dupont dips his paw in black ink and makes his mark on a piece of paper. It means you're on his hit list."

"He plans to assassinate you too?" said Oz, horrified.

"Uh-huh," said Glory. "It scared me—"

"Something like that would scare anyone!"

"—and I got distracted. During a mission that afternoon, one of Dupont's aides infiltrated the museum and almost got the Kiss of Death away from me."

"You mean that lipstick pistol on display upstairs in the Top Secret exhibit?"

Glory nodded.

"What were you doing with that?"

Glory sat up. She wiped away her tears with a paw. "One of our main objectives at the Spy Mice Agency, where I work—" she stopped abruptly and swallowed hard, "where I *used* to work, I mean, is to keep anything that could be used as a weapon against us out of rat paws. As new gadgets arrive, we field agents go in and retrieve them. Our lab replicates them at night with stuff from the Foragers' Cupboard. The Foragers are mice who collect things that you humans drop or throw away. Next morning—voila!—an undetectable fake."

Oz nodded thoughtfully. "So the Kiss of Death in the display case upstairs isn't the real thing?"

"Nope," said Glory. "Just an old lipstick somebody tossed in the ladies' room trash. The Foragers found it, and our lab mice doctored it up a bit to make it look like the real one."

Oz thought this over. Somehow it all made perfect sense. "So how come you got fired? I thought you said the rats *almost* got the Kiss of Death away from you."

Glory sighed. "Almost as of last Tuesday, but last night was another story. See, yesterday morning there was a glitch with another retrieval mission. Just a brief sighting by a human. It shouldn't have been a big deal, but Fumble tattled."

"Who's Fumble?"

"A stupid house mouse I work with. He's always on my tail about something. My brother B-Nut says he's just jealous, but for whatever reason, he has it in for me. Anyway, he told Julius, my boss. What with my father's assassination and now the Black Paw, Julius thinks the rats are up to something. He warned me that I was getting careless. Said three strikes and I was out."

"And last night was strike three?" guessed Oz.

"Big time." Glory heaved a sigh. "All I had to do was deliver the Kiss of Death to the British Embassy and go straight back to Central Command. But when I spotted Dupont, I figured I'd better see what he was up to. And then the Kiss of Death slipped out of my backpack and Dupont got it and almost got me and then I got fired."

Glory finished her tale of woe in a rush and slumped back into Oz's hand. She covered her face with her paws and began to cry again. "What's worse is I'm really, really scared," she said, sobbing. "I don't want to die, Oz! The Black Paw was bad enough, but now there'll be rat snipers crawling all over this city. I won't be safe anywhere! And it's all my own fault!"

Oz reached out a finger and stroked her fur soothingly. "It's not your fault, Glory. Everybody makes mistakes."

"Not like this one."

"Is there no way to get the Kiss of Death back?" Oz asked.

Glory shook her head. "Dupont is a tough customer,"

she said, sniffling. "I'd never seen him up close before until last night. He—he—"

"Did he do this to you?" Oz asked, brushing his fingertip against the bandage on Glory's shoulder.

Glory nodded. "He's evil, Oz," she whispered. "He's big, and he's mean, and he's really, really scary. No mouse has ever infiltrated his lair and lived to tell the tale. My father tried, and look what happened to him. Julius is sending in a team of commandos and elite agents tomorrow to try anyway." She sat up and wiped her nose with her tail. "No use crying over spilt milk, I guess. I'll just have to find another job and move someplace far, far away, where Dupont will never find me. Cincinnati, maybe. Or Tahiti." She looked over at Oz. "So what did you need to see me for? Your note said it was life or death."

Oz prodded at his glasses. His own predicament seemed pretty stupid now, in comparison to all that Glory was up against, but he explained about the sharks and the masquerade party anyway.

"I know the type," said Glory, when Oz finished describing Jordan and Tank. "Fumble, with a little Dupont thrown in." She hopped down off Oz's palm and paced back and forth across his knee. "Hmmmm," she said, her bright little eyes narrowing in concentration.

"Too bad you couldn't find a way to even the score. If you could, maybe you'd get this Jordan and Tank off your tail—er, so to speak—permanently."

"What if you got the Kiss of Death back?" said Oz suddenly. "You'd be safe then—well, safer. And maybe Julius would give you your job back."

Glory stopped in her tracks. She stared at him. "Me, infiltrate rat headquarters?

"Just a thought," said Oz.

"I couldn't do it on my own," said Glory. "I'd need help."

Boy and mouse regarded each other thoughtfully.

"Maybe we could help each other," suggested Oz.

"I was just thinking the same thing," said Glory.

"Hey, Oz! Where are you? Did you fall in? Your grilled cheese is stone cold!" D. B.'s voice came floating down the hallway.

Glory froze. Oz pulled off his baseball cap and casually placed it over his knee, shielding her from view.

"It's okay," he whispered. "It's just D. B."

"What's a D. B.?" Glory whispered back.

"Not a what, a who. Delilah Bean. She's my friend. The sharks are after her, too."

Glory hesitated. She'd taken a tremendous risk breaking the Mouse Code and talking to Oz. She didn't know this D. B. from a mouse hole in the wall. What if the girl screamed and ran? The Exterminator would be brought in for sure.

"I don't know, Oz," she whispered.

"Trust me, it'll be fine."

What can they do, fire me again? thought Glory bitterly. She took a deep breath. "In for a penny, in for a pound," she said.

"Great," said Oz. "You won't be sorry."

"Talking to yourself, Oz?" D. B. crouched down by the stairs. "What are you doing under there anyway?"

Oz looked over at his classmate. He poked at his glasses, which had slipped down his nose again. "D. B., can I trust you?"

She squinted at him. "Maybe."

"No maybes. It's gotta be a hundred percent."

D. B. shrugged. "Okay, you can trust me a hundred percent."

"Promise?"

"Yeah, I promise."

Oz was suddenly struck by fear. "How do I know I can trust you?" What if D. B. couldn't keep a secret? What if she told? When it came right down to it, despite his assurances to Glory, he hardly knew D. B.

D. B. stood up. She placed her hands on her hips

and tapped her foot. She looked at him, her lips pursed in a frown. "It's that important to you?"

Oz nodded vigorously.

D. B. shrugged. "Okay," she said. "Here goes. For starters, you can trust me because I know a lot more about you than you think. Stuff that I haven't told anybody."

Oz was surprised to hear this. "What kind of stuff?"

"Like, for instance, what it's like to have a famous mother and have everybody make fun of you because of it," D. B. replied. "Your mom's an opera singer, mine's on TV. Every single night. People have been teasing me because of her job since kindergarten."

Oz grunted. "Okay," he admitted grudgingly. "What else do you know?"

D. B. gave him a slow smile. "I know that your real name is Ozymandias."

Oz blinked at her in disbelief. "Who told you?"

"My mother's a reporter," said D. B. "She knows how to get information. Actually, your dad told her when she was here last month, but don't worry, I haven't said a word to anybody. I can imagine the mileage Jordan and Tank would get out of that, and I wouldn't sic those morons on anybody." D. B. shook her head in disgust. "What were your parents thinking?

I mean, it's a cool poem and everything, but it's a stupid name for a kid. I'd want to be just Oz too if I were you."

Oz couldn't believe D. B. had been sitting on this prime bit of information for a whole month. She could have blackmailed him. She could have sold him out to the sharks a hundred times over. "Okay," he said. "I trust you."

D. B. crouched down again. "So what's the big secret?"

"Well, there's this mouse, see, who's a spy," Oz began. "She works here at the museum. Not for the museum, actually. For the Spy Mice Agency." He stopped. He was putting this badly.

D. B. eyed him doubtfully. "A mouse?" she said. "Here at the museum? Who's a spy?" She grabbed him by the arm. "Whoa, buddy. Your blood sugar must be low. Better get you some lunch. There's no such thing as spy mice."

Oz slowly lifted the baseball cap off his knee. Glory stood motionless. *If I run for it now,* she thought, *I could probably make a clean getaway.* Instead, she waved.

D. B.'s mouth dropped open.

Oz grinned. "Delilah Bean, meet Morning Glory Goldenleaf."

CHAPTER 11

DAY TWO—
SATURDAY
1215 HOURS

"I do not believe I am having
this conversation," said D. B. flatly
a short while later. "I do not believe
I am talking to a *mouse*."

"A mouse who needs our help," said Oz.

"We're the ones who are going to need help if your
dad finds us here," said D. B., glancing over her shoulder at the café's back entrance.

"And I'm toast if anyone spots me talking to you
two," said Glory.

Oz placed his hand, palm upward, beside her again.
"Then there's just one thing to do," he said. "You'll
have to come home with me. Both of you," he added,
nodding at D. B. "We can talk in private there."

Glory hopped onto Oz's hand and he tucked her
into the breast pocket of his polo shirt. He stowed her

gear—skateboard, helmet, and backpack—safely in the pocket of his jeans, then followed D. B. back into the café.

"There you are, my little gingersnap," said his father as he slid into the booth. "I was beginning to worry about you."

Oz took a bite of his grilled cheese—still good, even if it was cold. "Is it okay with you if D. B. and I go back to our house to hang out for a while?"

"Fine with me if it's fine with D. B.'s mother," replied his father. He turned to D. B. "Why don't you give her a call? You can use the phone in the kitchen."

He glanced at the clock on the wall as D. B. scooted out of the booth. "If you can wait five minutes while I finish up here, I can drive you partway. I have to pick up a few things for tomorrow night's party from the caterers in Georgetown."

A few minutes later, Oz's father dropped them off in front of Thomas Sweet, the ice cream shop at the corner of Wisconsin and P Streets. Oz gazed longingly through the window. Bittersweet—a dark chocolate confection that was his favorite flavor—was calling to him.

D. B. plucked at his sleeve. "Not now, Oz," she said crossly.

Oz moved reluctantly past the shop and led them

toward Q Street. As soon as they were away from the busy foot traffic of Wisconsin, he tapped lightly on his shirt pocket. "You can come out now," he whispered to Glory.

Her elegant little nose popped out, followed by two bright little eyes. "Hey, I know where we are," Glory said, looking around. "This is my neighborhood."

"Really?" Oz was surprised. "You live in Georgetown? I thought you lived at the Spy Museum."

Glory gave a tiny snort. "Why would I live there? Do humans live where they work?"

"Well, no, I just thought—"

"You have a lot to learn about mice," said Glory. "I commute, just like everyone else."

"What, now you're telling me mice ride the Metro?" asked D. B.

"No, we leave that to the rats. We use Pigeon Air."

Oz and D. B. craned their heads back and stared up at the sky.

"Really?" said Oz.

"Only way to fly," Glory replied. She began to bounce excitedly. "There it is! There's my home!"

She waved a paw toward a heavy wrought-iron gate. The words DUMBARTON OAKS 1920 were picked out along it in gilded curlicues, along with interwoven patterns of

gilded leaves and acorns. Behind the gate's black bars a long gravel drive swept up toward a grand mansion surrounded by formal gardens.

"You live in a mansion?" exclaimed Oz. "Cool!"

"Not the house, you goose, that oak tree there, just inside the gate," Glory said. "Goldenleafs have lived there for hundreds of years."

Oz turned and pointed at a brick townhouse directly across the street. "You're not going to believe it, but that's *my* house right over there. Glory, we're neighbors."

D. B. was still staring at the oak tree. "So do you live in the tree all by yourself?"

"Heck no," said Glory. "I live there with my mother and father—" Her voice faltered slightly. "With my mother, I mean. And my brothers and sisters."

"How many of you are there?"

"Let's see," said Glory. "There's six of us in the muffin batch, and the four cookies—Snickerdoodle, Macaroon, Hermit, and Brownie—and Truffle and Taffy, the babies. That makes an even dozen of us now. Used to be seventeen, though, before the French pastries moved out. They're all grown up."

"Seventeen?" Oz gave a low whistle.

"French pastries?" added D. B., with a puzzled look.

"Croissant, Éclair, Petit Four, Napoleon, and Chantilly," explained Glory. "It's a Goldenleaf thing. My mother's from the Bakery Guild. She named all of us after sweets."

D. B. raised her eyebrows. "And I thought it was bad being named after my great-aunt."

Inside the Levinsons' townhouse, Oz set Glory down on the kitchen counter and popped a plate of frozen cookies into the microwave. "They're best when the chocolate chips are gooey," he said.

"Just the way I like them," Glory agreed.

Oz poured milk for himself and D. B., and rustled up a thimble for Glory. "So," he began, pulling up a stool. "Where exactly is Dupont's headquarters?"

Glory, who was perched on the edge of the cookie plate, took a sip of milk from the thimble and wiped her whiskers delicately with the corner of a napkin. "The entrance is under a bench at the Dupont Circle Metro station," she replied. "That much we know for sure. My father was the last mouse to try to infiltrate—he led a Mouse Guard commando squad on a special mission last July. They were ambushed. The others got out safely, but my father . . . my father . . ."

Her voice trailed off. Glory stared down at her cookie. "Dupont mailed us his tail," she whispered.

"That's horrible!" cried D. B.

Glory nodded. "It *was* horrible. My poor mother . . ." Again, her voice trailed off.

"And now you're on his hit list," said Oz, looking at Glory's own little tail with concern. "Glory, I don't think you should go through with this. Not with the Black Paw hanging over you. You're marked for death! It's far too dangerous. Couldn't we just toss some rat poison down there?"

"Dupont's stupid, but he's not that stupid," said Glory. "Every rat in D.C. knows about rat poison. No, I have to go in. Unless I get the Kiss of Death back, how am I ever going to feel safe again?"

Oz prodded at his glasses with his finger, leaving a chocolate blotch on one of the lenses. He sighed. "Well, if you're determined to go, I guess we can't stop you. We need to figure out a way to get you in and out safely."

The three of them were quiet for a while, the only sound the munching of chocolate chip cookies.

"I've got it—how about a disguise?" suggested D. B. "Like at that workshop this morning. We could dress Glory up as a rat."

Oz eyed Glory dubiously. "She'd be the smallest rat in history. Have you seen some of the bruisers patrolling the Metro tracks?"

"I agree," said Glory. "Dupont would sniff me out in a heartbeat."

The three of them were quiet again for a bit. Then D. B. sat bolt upright.

"The Trojan Horse!" she said.

Oz and Glory looked at her blankly.

"What?" said Oz.

"The Trojan Horse! From your social studies report, Oz, remember? It's perfect." She ran to the front hallway, where she had left her backpack, and brought it to the kitchen. D. B. pulled out the fake soda can she'd purchased at the Spy Museum gift shop. "It's just the right size for Glory," she pointed out, unscrewing the top. "We just need to poke a few airholes here and there, and roll her in."

"Hey, that's not a bad idea," said Oz, taking the can from her and inspecting it. "But how do we get her out again?"

D. B. bit her lip. Glory stroked her tail. Oz took another bite of cookie. The three of them were quiet again as they considered this.

"My father's old fishing rod might do the trick," Oz ventured.

D. B. looked at him as if he had two heads. "What?"

"You'll see," he said, darting through the basement

door. He returned again a minute later covered in cob-
webs and waving a dusty fishing rod. "Watch," he said,
unreeling a piece of transparent line from the reel. "We
tape this end to the can—duct tape should work—then
roll her in. When Glory's ready to go, we reel her back
out."

Glory leaped off the cookie plate. "It just might
work," she said, her whiskers beginning to twitch in
excitement. She crawled inside the soda can. "Yes," she
said, her voice echoing tinnily, "there's definitely
enough room in here for me and the Kiss of Death." She
crawled back out again and began to hop up and down
along the counter. "Oz, D. B., this is a stroke of genius!"

"But how will we know when Glory's ready for us to
pull her out?" said D. B.

Glory stopped hopping. Oz looked crestfallen. The
three of them were quiet again.

"Unless," Oz suggested, "we can figure out a way to
rig the soda can with a transmitter or something."

At this, a slow smile spread across Glory's face.
"That's easy," she said. "I know just the mouse for the
job."

CHAPTER 12

DAY TWO—
SATURDAY
1430 HOURS

"I do not believe I am seeing this," said D. B. The three of them were up in Oz's room, sitting at his desk. "I do not believe that mice know how to use computers."

Glory grinned, flipping neatly through the air from the B key to the U key on the keyboard. "Hey, I'm a trained professional," she said. "I used to do this for a living."

Oz and D. B. watched in amazement as Glory leaped and twirled and somersaulted expertly from one letter to the next. A message began to appear on the screen:

From: glory@tailmail.com

To: bunsen@spymiceagency.com

Re: Top Secret—For Your Paws Only—Urgent

    Bunsen, I'm in trouble. I desperately need your help.

> Can you meet me at the Spy Mice Agency entrance at
> 1530 hours? Don't let anyone know about this, and
> don't let anyone see you. Especially not Fumble.

Glory bounced back and forth across the keyboard as she continued the message, listing the items that she wanted to borrow.

"There," she said with satisfaction as she made one final soaring acrobatic leap and pressed "Send." "That should take care of things."

"This Bunsen of yours, will he do it?" asked D. B. "Will he help us?"

Glory cocked her head, considering. "Bunsen is true blue," she replied finally. "A real pal. He'll help."

"So that solves your problem, but what about ours?" asked Oz. "We still need to figure out what to do about Jordan and Tank."

"I'm working on that," said Glory, nibbling on a chocolate chip. "You say he'll be at the party tomorrow night?"

Oz nodded. "For sure. He and Tank are all fired up about it. I heard them talking on the bus."

"Perfect," said Glory. "That gives us the opportunity—now we just need a plan of action." Her brow furrowed in concentration, she took another nibble of chocolate chip. Suddenly, she started to laugh. It was a delightful sound, like the pealing of a very small silver bell, and Oz and D. B. both smiled.

"Oh, that would be fun," Glory said. "Risky, but fun."

"What?" asked D. B.

Glory ignored her. She began to pace up and down across Oz's desk, chuckling and talking to herself. "Couldn't do it all on my own, though. At least I don't think I could. Hmmm. That could be a problem. Still, maybe there's a way—" She stopped and gave Oz and D. B. a speculative glance.

"I think I've got an idea for the trap. But I need some way to get Jordan and Tank to a specific spot at a specific time tomorrow night at the party. I need some bait."

Oz looked at D. B. D. B. looked at Oz. They both sighed.

"That would be us," said D. B. Her smile had vanished, and she sounded cross.

"Right," said Glory breezily. "You two are the bait."

"Surprise, surprise," muttered D. B. under her breath.

"You have to be disguised, though," said Glory, continuing to ignore her. "From what Oz has told me, Jordan and Tank are a lot like Dupont—stupid, but crafty. If they recognize you right away, they may get suspicious. Or they might pounce too soon."

"I was planning on going as James Bond," said Oz in a shy voice.

D. B.'s eyes widened in surprise. "Really?"

Oz reddened. "It's just a costume," he mumbled defensively.

"No, I didn't mean—I only meant—that's awesome." D. B. sounded flustered. "Double-O-Seven is my favorite spy too."

Oz gave her a sidelong glance. "Yeah, he's cool," he admitted, adding in a low tone, "a lot cooler than I'll ever be." He dropped his gaze and fiddled with his napkin.

Glory looked at Oz, her bright little eyes full of sympathy. "Oh, I don't know, Oz," she said softly. "I'd say you have all the makings of an excellent spy."

Oz looked up. "Really?"

Glory nodded. "Sure. You're smart, you're observant, you know how to keep a secret. Brave too. It takes a lot of guts to start all over at a new school year after year, and that's not counting the sharks." Oz gave her a grateful smile. "However," Glory continued briskly, "the tuxedo thing won't work at all. Not this time around, Oz. You need to be completely unrecognizable."

"That's not going to be easy," said Oz unhappily, gazing down at himself. "I'm pretty hard to hide."

The three of them were quiet again. Then Oz blurted out, "The Trojan Horse!"

D. B. stared at him. "You're going to go as a soda can?"

Oz shook his head impatiently. "No, but the whole soda can thing's given me an idea." He held out his hand and Glory climbed onto his palm. "I need to call Australia."

CHAPTER 13

DAY TWO—
SATURDAY
1530 HOURS

"I'm still not sure about this," said Bunsen. "I could lose my job if anyone caught me lending you this stuff from Deep Freeze."

"I know you could, Bunsen, but you're the only mouse I can trust right now," Glory replied. "Everyone else will try and stop me."

"Which is exactly what I should do," said Bunsen, his whiskers quivering in disapproval. "Dupont's lair! Glory, you must be crazy. He sent you the *Black Paw*! It's far too dangerous."

"Dangerous times call for dangerous measures," countered Glory. "It could mean all-out war if we don't get that Kiss of Death back. I, for one, will never be safe again. The last I saw of your homing device, Bunsen, it was strung around Dupont's neck. Can't you track him from Central Command and keep me posted on his whereabouts? That way he won't be able to sneak up on me."

Bunsen crossed his paws on his chest. "Track him from Central Command? You *are* crazy, Glory! If you do go in, it has to be a solo mission. Unauthorized. Off the radar screen. I can't be caught monitoring you from Central Command. That homing device is useless to us now." He began to pace. "I still don't think you should be attempting this on your own. Julius is sending in a special recovery team tomorrow morning. Can't you just let them take care of it?"

"I lost it—it's my responsibility to get it back," said Glory stubbornly. "And when I do, Julius will have to give me my job back. Anyway," she added, scuffing a paw on the hallway floor and giving Bunsen a sidelong glance. "I'm not entirely alone."

Her colleague breathed a sigh of relief. "Well, that at least is good news!" he said. "So B-Nut is going with you then?"

Glory shook her head. "Nooooo. Not B-Nut."

"Hank?"

Glory shook her head again.

"Who, then?"

"Bunsen, if I tell you this, you have to promise you

won't turn me in," Glory said, taking his paw in hers and giving him a pleading look.

Bunsen glanced down at their intertwined paws and blushed a warm shade of pink that spread from the tip of his nose to the tip of his snowy white tail. "Well I, I—" he stammered, then stopped. "Turn you in?" He looked at Glory suspiciously. "Glory, what have you done?"

Glory dropped his paw. She hung her head.

Bunsen was aghast. "Glory, you don't mean to say, you didn't, you haven't—oh Glory, you haven't spoken to *humans*!"

"But they're *good* humans, Bunsen, honestly they are!" Glory burst out defiantly. "True blue. And almost as smart as mice. You'll like them."

"Like them! Glory, you broke the Mouse Code!" Bunsen tugged on his ears unhappily. "This just keeps getting worse," he moaned. He paced up and down again, wringing his paws. "I'll be fired now, too, I just know it. I'll end up polishing test tubes at Uncle Fahrenheit's lab back in Baltimore."

"Bunsen," said Glory sharply. "Get a grip. No one is going to find out."

The slim white mouse drew himself up to his full height. "There's only one thing to be done," he said. "I'm going with you."

Glory blinked at him in surprise. "But Bunsen, you're a lab mouse! I mean, it's very sweet of you to offer, but really, I can handle this by myself."

"No, I insist," said Bunsen. "Otherwise, the deal's off and the equipment goes back to storage."

"Aw, come on, Bunsen! You've never gone out in the field before! You don't have the training for this kind of thing!"

Bunsen looked hurt. "It's not as if I don't have a brain," he said.

"I didn't meant to insult you—"

"Besides, you're going to need technical support. That at least is entirely clear." Ignoring Glory's protests, Bunsen pulled a large baby sock duffel bag out from the shadows and opened it. "Let's see, transmitter, check. Field agent regulation microphone and earpiece, check. Tool kit, check."

"Oh, very well then," said Glory, a bit crossly. "Let me just get Oz and D. B."

Bunsen straightened up, his pink eyes widening in fear. "You mean the humans are here? Now?"

"It'll be fine, Bunsen, trust me." Glory gave a sharp whistle.

Oz and D. B. poked their heads out from the café's back entrance. As they approached the mice, Bunsen began to tremble. Glory placed a comforting paw on his shoulder.

"Bunsen, meet Oz—his father runs the café—and D. B. They're friends of mine," she finished, emphasizing the word "friends."

"I'm, uh, pleased to meet you," squeaked Bunsen. "I think."

Oz and D. B. squatted down by the pile of gadgets heaped on the floor.

"What *is* this stuff?" asked D. B. scornfully, poking at the items with her finger. "Looks like something from my grandfather's junk drawer."

"The equipment may be old," Bunsen replied stiffly, "but it's still serviceable. In fact, better than serviceable. We in the lab have made a few, um, improvements. Mouse technology may not be quite as advanced as yours—yet—but you needn't twitch your whiskers at it."

"I think the correct human expression is, 'turn up your nose at it,'" whispered Glory.

"I still say it looks old as the hills," said D. B.

"A bit dated, perhaps," Bunsen conceded.

"Dated?" scoffed D. B. "This stuff hasn't been dusted off since World War Two."

"There's no need to be snippy about it," the lab

mouse huffed. "I can promise you it will work all right. I will admit that your computer microchip is proving a tough nut to crack, but we have lab mice working around the clock on the problem. Radio technology, however, is quite simple and nearly foolproof—" He paused and looked down at the duffel bag in dismay. "Radio technology! What are we going to use for a receiver? Now that this is an undercover solo mission, you can't transmit back to Central Command as usual."

"Oh, dear," said Glory. "That is a problem."

Bunsen began rummaging through the duffel bag in a panic. "There's this, and well, no, I couldn't use that. Let me see here, how about . . ."

"You need a radio?" said Oz.

"Not exactly," Bunsen replied. His voice was muffled, as his head was now entirely inside the duffel bag. "I need a receiver."

Oz cleared his throat. He held up his CD player. "Could you use this?"

Bunsen pulled his head out of the duffel bag. His pink eyes lit up when he saw what Oz held in his hand. "I've read about these, but I've never actually seen one up close," he said in excitement, hopping over for a better look. "The Foragers haven't had any luck acquiring one yet." Oz laid it down on the floor so the mouse could inspect it more closely. Bunsen grabbed a tiny screwdriver (foraged from an eyeglasses repair kit) from his duffel bag and expertly unscrewed the back.

"Yes," he said. "Yes, I think I can make this work."

Glory winked at Oz. "See? I told you that you had all the makings of a secret agent." She turned to Bunsen. "The boy can think on his paws. His feet, I mean."

Oz gazed modestly at his shoes, but he couldn't keep a smile from creeping across his face. As Bunsen busied himself converting the CD player to a radio receiver, Oz squatted down and poked idly through the gadgets again.

"Hey, what's this?"

Glory scurried over to see what he had found. "The watch camera!" she said, frowning. "That wasn't on my list, Bunsen."

"Oh, I brought along several things that weren't on your list," said Bunsen airily. "One never knows. You might want to take a few pictures of Dupont's lair. If you make it that far," he added gloomily.

"Oh, I'll make it that far all right," said Glory, whose tail was beginning to flutter in excitement. "Good thinking, Bunsen. Pictures of Rat HQ. That'll wow Julius. He can't help but give me my job back then."

"Eeeew, what's that?" said D. B., pointing to a small brown lump in the pile.

"That is a transmitter," explained Bunsen. "Not on Glory's list either, but I thought that if there were room for it in the soda can—the, ah, Trojan Horse, as you put it—we might use it to bug Dupont's headquarters."

"Bunsen! That's brilliant!" cried Glory, and the lab mouse's nose glowed pink with pleasure.

"It looks like dog doo," D. B. protested.

"It's *supposed* to look like dog doo," said Bunsen.

"That is disgusting," stated D. B., folding her arms across her chest.

"It's just plastic," said Oz, picking it up. "See?"

D. B. shuddered. "I still say it's disgusting."

"We do not have time to be arguing over dog doo!" said Glory, tapping a paw on the hallway floor in irritation. "We have a long afternoon ahead of us."

"Almost done here," said Bunsen, replacing the cover on the back of the CD player and tightening it down again.

As Bunsen packed the gear back into his duffel bag and climbed into Oz's pocket next to Glory—not without a few squeaks of apprehension, for the lab mouse had never been this close to a human before—no one noticed the plump nose that appeared in the mouse hole entrance to the Spy Mice Agency. Nor did they notice as Fumble quietly observed their preparations, then just as quietly withdrew into the darkness.

CHAPTER 14

DAY TWO—
SATURDAY
1600 HOURS

"What's a rat have to do to get a decent meal around here?"

Dupont was in a foul mood again. He stuck his snout into a grease-stained pizza box and snuffled hopefully. Finding nothing but a single anchovy and a thin smear of mozzarella cheese, he withdrew his snout again and gave a snort of disgust. "Useless trash. Lulu!"

Limburger Lulu came scurrying out of the shadows. "Yes, Boss?"

Dupont glared at her. "I need food, FOOD! Sustenance! Haven't I made that clear? Find that worthless brother of yours and tell him if he doesn't get his worthless tail in gear and bring me something to eat pronto, and I mean *pronto*, I'll be putting HIM on the menu!"

Lulu squeaked in terror. "Yes, Boss!" she said, and scurried off into the shadows again.

"Gnaw! Scurvy!"

Dupont's scruffy aides materialized instantly. "Yes, sir?"

"What's the latest on the Goldenleaf brat? Have you found her yet?"

Gnaw scratched his lone ear fearfully. He hated to be the bearer of bad tidings. Especially to Roquefort Dupont. "Disappeared," he finally managed to whisper.

"What? Speak up, you useless sewer crawler."

"She disappeared," repeated Gnaw in a marginally louder croak.

"DISAPPEARED?!" roared Dupont, and Gnaw nearly leapt out of his fur. "What do you mean, 'disappeared'?"

"We were watching all the entrances to the museum, had the roof covered and the gate to Dumbarton Oaks and everything," Gnaw babbled. "There's been absolutely no sign of her. She vanished into thin air."

"Maybe they moved her to a safe house," ventured Scurvy.

His boss turned on him. "If I want your opinion I'll ask for it," he snarled, and Scurvy drew back in alarm. Dupont started to pace. "Vanished, you say?"

"Yes, boss," said Gnaw.

"You see that wall?" Dupont said, booting a petrified nectarine pit across his litter-strewn headquarters. It bounced off the far wall and skittered into the shadows.

Gnaw eyed the wall. Upon it were nailed a number of small, shriveled, and decidedly unsavory objects. He nodded unhappily. "Yes, sir."

"Have you forgotten about the WALL?" roared Dupont, whipping his tail back and forth angrily.

Gnaw shook his head vigorously. "No, sir!"

"See that you don't," barked Dupont, lurching across his lair. He stared up at the expanse of dank stone and squinted at his trophies. "Now, was it this one or that one?" he muttered. "Ah, there it is."

He tapped a dried flap of gray fur with his tail and turned, casting a speculative glance at his aide's remaining ear. Gnaw placed a paw protectively over it and shrank back. "I left room for the other one right beside it," Dupont said in a silky tone. "In fact, it's looking a little lonely tonight, don't you think, up here all by itself."

He advanced toward Gnaw, who cowered against a greasy brown lunch bag. "That's right," murmured Dupont, still advancing. "Fear is good. Fear and terror.

Those are a rat's best weapons." He bared his yellowed fangs at Gnaw. "Shall we just have it off right here and now, then? Relieve you of the suspense once and for all?" Dupont gave a brutal laugh, then snapped his razor-sharp teeth together with a *CLACK!* that made Gnaw leap skyward again.

"Incompetent nincompoop!" said Dupont in disgust, turning away. "Get out of my sight. And don't come back until you have that Goldenleaf brat! She can't have vanished—she's out there somewhere. Turn up the heat. You'll find her."

Gnaw didn't have to be told twice. As he scuttled off, Dupont picked up the Kiss of Death and stroked it lovingly. He turned to Scurvy. "Anything else to report? How about upstairs? Any unusual activity?"

"Nothing," Scurvy replied. "Just a couple of kids parked on our bench waiting for their train."

"Good," said Dupont, rubbing his paws together. "And is everything set for tomorrow night?"

Scurvy nodded. "The troops are gathered in the sewer right now, awaiting your speech."

Dupont bared his yellowed teeth again in a smile. "Then let's give them what they came for, shall we? LULU! LOUIE!"

The rats-in-waiting, who had been watching the

proceedings with trepidation, jumped as they heard their names and tumbled tail over whiskers across the lair to land in a heap at Dupont's paws. They lay there, trembling.

Dupont's smile was a soulless grimace as he gazed down at the two of them. "It's showtime!" he whispered. "Just as soon as you bring me something to EAT!"

CHAPTER 15

DAY TWO—
SATURDAY
16:15 HOURS

"Agent in place."

Glory's voice crackled over Oz's headphones. Oz turned the volume up slightly and gave Bunsen and D. B., who were seated next to him on the bench in the Metro station, a thumbs-up. "She's in," he reported.

"Can she see anything?" Bunsen asked.

"Glory, can you see anything?" Oz relayed the question.

For a moment there was only silence, then Glory's voice came floating through the headphones again. "I see it," she said, a note of triumph in her voice. "Propped up against a cottage cheese container."

"What else does she see?" prompted Bunsen. "Is Dupont there?"

Oz relayed the question to Glory, who replied, "Yeah, and Scurvy is with him."

"How about the Limburger twins?"

"No sign of them, or of Gnaw. I'll sit tight and wait until the coast is clear, then I'm going in."

Bunsen clutched his pale paws together when Oz told him Glory's reply. "Oh, do tell her to be careful!" he said. "I don't think I could bear it if something happened to her—but don't tell her that part," he added hastily.

As Oz relayed the first part of Bunsen's message, D. B. gave the slender white mouse a speculative glance. "So Bunsen, does that mean what I think it means?"

Bunsen's nose and tail turned bright pink. He sighed. "No use trying to hide it, I suppose. Glory Goldenleaf is the most amazing creature I've ever seen. She's beautiful, and brave, and clever—and I don't stand a chance."

"Why not?"

"Because I'm a lab mouse, of course," said Bunsen matter-of-factly.

"What's wrong with being a lab mouse?" asked D. B.

Bunsen drooped. "It's so ordinary," he lamented. "So dull. What could a mouse like Glory possibly see in a scientific mouse like me? I'm sure she goes for the more glamorous type—a real mouse-about-town. One of those explorers from the National Geographic Society, perhaps, or a hotshot Silver Skateboard agent, or a dashing surveillance pilot. Not a plodder like me."

"I'd hardly call you a plodder," said D. B. "Besides, you're the one Glory turned to for help, aren't you?"

Bunsen gave a dismissive wave of his paw. "That's just because I could get her all this equipment."

"You shouldn't write yourself off so quickly," D. B. insisted. "You've got a lot going for you, Bunsen. You're smart too and brave. You talked to us humans, didn't you? And I'm sure you're very good-looking—for a mouse."

Bunsen blushed again. Ducking his head bashfully, he twiddled the dials on the makeshift radio receiver. Oz nudged D. B.

"I do not believe you are having this conversation," he whispered. "I do not believe you are talking to a mouse about his love life."

D. B. grinned. The headphones crackled again, and the three of them sprang to attention.

"Dupont and Gnaw are heading off," said Glory. "The coast is clear. Tell Bunsen I'll hide the dog-doo receiver in a safe spot, take a few pictures, then grab the Kiss of Death. Be ready to pull me out when I give the signal. I may be moving fast."

"Roger that," said Oz, hoping he sounded a little bit like James Bond. He pressed the headphones tightly to his ears, listening intently. Bunsen was perched in his pocket, anxiously clutching his tail. D. B. grasped the fishing rod with both hands. The three of them sat on the bench, motionless, waiting for Glory's signal.

Two subway trains came and went. A couple with a baby in a stroller wandered by and glanced at them curiously. Oz started bobbing his head back and forth, pretending to listen to music on his headphones. D. B. made a show of examining her fingernails. The couple walked on.

"NOW!"

Oz jerked upright, Glory's command ringing in his ears.

"Now!" he cried.

D. B. started reeling Glory in, her small hand a blur as she wound the handle of the fishing reel. It wasn't long before they heard the clanking of the soda can as it clattered up the last few feet of the tunnel.

Oz reached under the bench and grabbed the can as it emerged from the hole marking the entrance to Dupont's lair.

"Open it up," said D. B.

"Hurry!" Bunsen urged.

Oz hastily unscrewed the lid. Glory emerged, and without a word she passed the Kiss of Death and the watch-camera to Bunsen, who stowed them both in Oz's pocket. Then she hauled herself up onto Oz's palm. She was shaking like a leaf.

"Glory, what is it? What's wrong?" cried Bunsen.

"My father," Glory whispered, her whiskers trembling uncontrollably.

"Your father?" Bunsen stared at her. "I don't understand."

Glory's bright little eyes brimmed with tears. "He's still alive."

Bunsen gasped.

"Barely, but he's alive," Glory continued. "Dupont has been keeping him in a cage."

Oz and D. B. exchanged a horrified glance. The flush of pink that had come to Bunsen's nose and tail at seeing his beloved safely back again drained away.

"Oh, Glory!" he said.

"It's horrible down there!" she continued, still quaking uncontrollably. "Dupont has a wall, a wall—" her voice broke.

"A wall?" Oz repeated, mystified.

"Of trophies," Glory managed to whisper. "Ears and tails. Hundreds of them."

The children and the lab mouse stared at her in shock.

"It's dreadful," Glory finished. "I've never seen anything like it. Dupont is a *monster*."

"What are we going to do?" asked D. B.

Glory drew a deep breath and squared her shoulders. "There's only one thing to do," she announced. "I'm going back for my father."

CHAPTER 16

DAY TWO—
SATURDAY
1630 HOURS

"Glory, you can't go back!" cried Bunsen in alarm. "It's a miracle you got out of there at all!"

"I can't just leave him there," Glory replied. "I won't. He's my father."

Bunsen's whiskers quivered in agitation. "Glory, this is a job for the Mouse Guard commandos, not for a solo field agent."

Glory shook her head stubbornly. "There's no time for that. When Dupont discovers that the Kiss of Death is gone, I'm the first one he'll suspect, and he may take it out on my father." She gave the three of them a pleading look. "Besides, the sooner I get him out, the better. He doesn't look so good."

Oz and D. B. and Bunsen were silent.

"Okay, Glory, we're behind you one hundred

percent," Oz said finally, speaking with a confidence he didn't feel. "We'll play it just like we did before. You go in, grab your dad, and we'll have you out of there in nothing flat."

Glory gave her friends a tremulous smile. "Thanks," she said. "You're all true blue." Shouldering her backpack, she gave a sharp nod. "Right, then. Let's roll."

Like a tiny astronaut entering a space capsule, Glory hopped from Oz's palm back into the soda can. She gave Oz and D. B. and Bunsen a quick salute, then crouched down in the silvery interior as Oz screwed the lid down tight.

"Good luck, Glory," he whispered through one of the airholes. His heart gave a twinge. Oz had known Glory for just a single day, but Bunsen was right—she was one of the bravest creatures he'd ever met.

D. B. released the catch on the fishing reel. The line whirred out as Oz tugged the soda can toward the hole beneath the bench.

"All systems go," he said into his microphone. "Are you ready?"

"Blast off," Glory replied.

Oz dropped the can into the hole and it rolled off into the darkness. The whir of the fishing line echoed in the cavernous subway station as it flew off the reel, and Oz glanced around to see if anyone noticed. None of the late afternoon travelers paid the two children—and one unseen lab mouse—the slightest bit of attention.

Glory was breathless and dizzy by the time the can finally clattered back into rat headquarters. It bumped up against the empty pizza box, rolled back and forth a few times, then came to a stop. She lay motionless inside, her heart pounding as she strained to hear Dupont and his cronies.

"Looks like Louie finally came through for you, boss," she heard Scurvy say. "He sent you a can of soda."

Glory sat up in a panic. She heard the scrabble of rat claws as someone crossed headquarters toward her hiding place. Her heart almost stopped beating altogether. They'd see the airholes!

And then, the can jerked and rolled again as someone gave it a kick. Inside, Glory rolled with it.

"I said something to EAT, not DRINK!" screeched Dupont. "If I was thirsty, I would have said so! Where is that worthless rat-in-waiting? Louie!"

Glory heard the click of Dupont's claws as he retreated, then silence. The seconds ticked by. Finally, she lifted her head and slowly, quietly inched toward the closest airhole. She peered out into the dim chamber.

"No sign of them," she whispered into her microphone. "I think they're gone."

"Be absolutely certain before you open that lid," ordered Oz, feeling more like James Bond by the moment.

"Roger," Glory replied, and crouched motionless for another excruciatingly long minute. Then, moving with painstaking care, she quietly unscrewed the lid to the can, pushed it aside a tiny crack, and peeped out. The lair was indeed empty; the only sign of rats was a lingering, unmistakable odor. Glory wrinkled her nose in distaste. It smelled like dirty gym socks and moldy cheese.

She set the soda can lid carefully aside and climbed out onto the pizza box lid. "Agent in place," she whispered. "I'm going to get my father."

Her earpiece crackled slightly, and then she heard Bunsen's voice. "Do be careful, Glory!"

"Don't worry, Bunsen. I'll be back in two shakes of a rat's tail. But just for the record, if anything happens to me, find B-Nut. He'll know what to do."

With that, Glory crept cautiously off toward the dark corner where she had seen the cage containing her father. She skirted a banana peel, skipped over a crust of peanut butter sandwich, and held her nose as she passed an open tuna can whose contents were covered with a thick layer of green fuzz.

Not wanting to startle her father, she tiptoed up to the cage. It was crudely fashioned from coat hangers and duct tape, and in the far corner sat Dumbarton Goldenleaf, his head slumped on his chest. His paws were manacled together behind his back and his fur was dull and matted. He looked awful. Glory gazed at the stump of his once-proud tail and a little sob escaped her.

"Pop!" she called softly. "Pop, wake up! It's me, Glory!"

There was no response. Was she too late? Fighting a rising panic, Glory called again to him, louder this time. "Pop! It's me, Glory!"

Dumbarton Goldenleaf's head tilted to the side, and one eye opened a crack. "Glory?" he said groggily. "My Glory?"

"Yes!" cried Glory in relief. "It's me, Pop! I've come to take you home."

With an effort, the general roused himself and swayed to his feet. "Dupont's not gone far," he warned. "Careful."

Glory nodded. "Hold on, Pop, I'll have you out in a whisker." She began to gnaw quietly at the duct tape that held the cage door shut. When she was through, she pulled open the door and hopped inside. "Let's get these handcuffs off you," she said, gently but swiftly untwisting the wire that held her father's paws pinned to the rungs of the cage. "There." Glory hugged her father, who hugged her back feebly. He was so frail!

"My brave Glory," he whispered.

She looked up at him. Her smile faltered. "Your ears!" she exclaimed.

"What about my ears?" asked her father.

"You still have them! Dupont told me he'd nailed them to, to—you know."

"His trophy wall?" Dumbarton Goldenleaf nodded grimly. "Oh, he was planning to, make no mistake. Almost did on several occasions. But Dupont enjoys stringing his victims along nearly as much as he does striking the final blow. Terror is the name of his game, Glory, fear and terror. There's only one weapon for dealing with those cowardly tactics, and that's courage. Don't you forget it."

"Let's get you out of here," said Glory, tugging on her father's paw.

Her father shook his head. "Dupont is up to something," he said. "I overheard him plotting. He and Scurvy headed down to the sewer just now for some kind of a rally. We need to find out their plans."

As Dumbarton Goldenleaf stumbled through the cage door, Glory put her paw around his waist to keep him from toppling over. Her father was weak and could barely walk. "The only thing we have to do is get you out of here," she said firmly.

"Glory, we must. Lives could depend on it."

She sighed. Goldenleafs and their sense of duty. It would be the end of them all one day. She, of all mice, however, understood. "Right, Pop. Let's go."

Leaning on his daughter for support, Dumbarton Goldenleaf limped down the dark corridor that led off from the south side of Dupont's lair. It sloped steadily downward as it neared the sewer, the walls turning from dank to downright slimy. The smell was, if possible, even worse than Dupont's garbage-strewn lair. A fetid odor wafted in from the distance to join the old-gym-socks-and-moldy-cheese scent of rat, and it was all Glory could do not to gag. What she wouldn't give to be back in her own home right now, the only smell that of the special apple pancakes her mother always made for Saturday night supper!

"I can hear them," she whispered. Her father nodded. Sure enough, in the distance a slow chanting could be heard, as a throng of rat voices joined in hailing Roquefort Dupont.

Glory and her father slowed their pace as they neared the entrance to the sewer. Dumbarton Goldenleaf finally stopped. He leaned back against the wall, exhausted. "You'll have to take it from here," he whispered. "I can't go another step."

Glory's father patted her weakly on the shoulder, and she crept forward to the entrance. Flattening herself into the shadows, she poked her head around the corner and peered into the gloom.

Thousands of red rat eyes gleamed back at her from the darkness. Row after row of them, as far into the distance as Glory could see. Rats clung to the wet walls; rats crouched in the shadows; rats floated in the shallows at the edge of the vast sewer. An immense army of rats, and all of their blazing red eyes fixed on her. Or so it seemed to Glory, whose bright little eyes widened in alarm for a split second—until she realized that they were not staring at her, but rather at their leader. For there on a ledge to her left, almost close enough to reach out and touch with her paw, stood Roquefort Dupont.

"Rats! Are you ready?" Dupont cried.

"Yes!" squeaked a thousand rat voices in reply, nearly deafening Glory. She clapped her paws over her ears.

"Have we had enough?"

"Yes!" came the thunderous reply.

"Are we ready to show those small-paws once and for all who owns this city?"

"Yes!"

Dupont was whipping the ranks into a frenzy. *Julius was right*, thought Glory in despair. *The rats were up to something.*

"In less than twenty-four hours, we move out," screeched Dupont, his raspy voice echoing weirdly off the sewer walls. "In less than twenty-four hours, we launch Operation P.E.S.T. Control!"

The assembled rats gave a mighty cheer. "Put an End to Short Tails!" they began to chant.

"Everyone who is anyone in this city will be at the Spy Museum tomorrow night," continued Dupont. "The movers and shakers of human and mouse society alike—senators and Council members, Supreme Court justices and the short-tails' own Judicial Guild, stars of stage and screen, the high-muckety-mucks of the Mouse Guard and every spy in the Spy Mice Agency's ranks!"

The rats cheered again.

"Your orders are clear," continued Dupont. "Swarm and surround!"

"Swarm and surround!" screamed his army in reply.

"The minute the humans spot us, they'll call in all the Exterminators in the city."

"Yes!" cried the rats in excitement, and started to chant, "Exterminate! Exterminate! Put an End to Short Tails!"

"That's right!" shrieked Dupont. "When the trucks arrive, that's our signal to disappear. The mice will be trapped inside. They won't stand a chance. And with their leaders taken out, all that lovely technology and all those lovely weapons will be ours! And with them, the entire city!"

"YES!" screamed the rats again. "EXTERMINATE! EXTERMINATE!"

Their chanting rose to a deafening pitch. Glory withdrew back around the corner. Her head was throbbing.

"Pop, did you hear that?" she gasped. "Did you hear what they're planning to do?"

Her father nodded weakly. "We must warn Julius and mobilize the Mouse Guard."

Glory put a paw around his waist and the two of them

hobbled back up the tunnel toward Dupont's lair. Behind them, rat voices were drawing closer. The rally was over.

"Hurry, Pop!" urged Glory. But her father's strength was drained by his months in captivity, and Glory had to practically carry him the last few steps to the soda can.

"Oz!" she said. "Are you there, Oz?"

"Affirmative," came the reply.

"On my signal." Glory pushed her father inside, then crawled in after him just as Dupont entered the lair. Scurvy was right on his tail.

"That went well," boasted Dupont. "I give a good speech, if I say so myself."

"Yes, Boss," his aide hurriedly agreed.

Glory quietly picked up the soda can lid and, moving with infinite care so as not to attract attention, began to screw it in place.

"Now maybe I can finally get something to eat," Dupont grumbled. Glory heard the sound of trash being kicked aside. "By the Black Paw, there's not so much as a single french fry around here. Louie! Lulu! Where *are* those worthless rats?"

Dupont drew closer on his hunt for food, and Glory froze. She motioned to her father to be silent. He nodded.

"Guess I might as well have something to quench my thirst while I'm waiting," Dupont announced, and lumbered over toward the soda can. It rolled back and forth as the enormous rodent nudged it with his snout. "Empty!" he said in disgust.

Glory peered through one of the airholes as Dupont started to move away. All of a sudden he paused, lifted his nose into the air, and sniffed. "What is that smell?" he demanded.

Scurvy lifted his nose into the air and sniffed as well. "I don't smell anything, Boss," he said.

"Are you sure?"

Scurvy nodded vigorously, which set his droopy whiskers flapping. "Positive."

Dupont's beady red eyes fixed on the soda can. They narrowed in suspicion, and Glory drew back quickly away from the airhole. "Scurvy, check the prisoner!" commanded Dupont.

Scurvy scuttled off into the shadows as the Sewer Lord padded slowly toward Glory and her father. The two of them crouched inside their hiding place, scarcely daring to breathe. Glory's father squeezed her paw. "Courage," he whispered. Glory nodded, but her heart was pounding wildly.

Scurvy scuttled back into the lair. "The prisoner's gone!" he cried.

"But not so very far, it would seem," said Dupont.

With a malevolent smile, he leaned toward the can and pressed his ugly snout up against an airhole. He inhaled deeply. Inside, Glory clutched her father's paw.

"Well, well, well," said Roquefort Dupont. "What have we here? While the rat's away, how the mice do play. Thought you could escape the Black Paw, General Goldenleaf? Think again."

CHAPTER 17

DAY TWO—
SATURDAY
16:45 HOURS

"NOW!" Glory shouted.

Oz jerked his head up in alarm as her cry blasted through his headphones.

"Reel her in!" he cried to D. B. "Hurry! Something's wrong!"

D. B. started reeling frantically. Oz could feel Bunsen's paws digging into his skin through the fabric of his shirt. "Is she all right?" the lab mouse asked anxiously.

"Shhh, I'm trying to find out," said Oz, pressing the headphones to his ears and closing his eyes in concentration. At first, he couldn't hear anything above the clattering of the soda can as it ricocheted back and forth along the tunnel, tugged upward by the fishing line. Then, in the background, he began to make out Dupont's voice.

"After them, you idiot!" he heard the rat shout in a rage. "Faster, they're getting away!"

"Dupont and Scurvy are chasing them," he reported tersely.

"Oh, do pull faster, D. B.!" Bunsen urged.

D. B.'s hand was practically a blur, her face set in lines of fierce determination as she worked to reel the soda can containing their friend and her father to safety.

"Hold on, Glory!" Oz shouted into the microphone. He gasped as another sharp cry from his tiny friend blasted through his headphones. All of a sudden, the fishing rod snapped up toward the ceiling and D. B. toppled backward off the bench. "Ouch!" she cried, landing hard on the concrete floor.

Oz rushed to help her up. "What happened?"

D. B. shook her head. "I don't know. One minute I could feel the weight of the can, and the next minute— nothing."

"Glory? Glory!" Oz shouted into the microphone. There was no response.

"Is she there?" cried Bunsen. "Check the line and see. Maybe D. B. is mistaken. She must be mistaken!"

Oz took the fishing rod from D. B. and reeled in the

last few feet of line. There was no soda can attached to the end of it.

He stared down at it, then at Bunsen and D. B. The three of them looked at each other in horror.

"What do we do now?" asked D. B.

CHAPTER 18

DAY TWO—
SATURDAY
1645 HOURS

Roquefort Dupont held up the piece of severed fishing line. His ugly rat mouth curved into a malicious grin.

"Nice going, Scurvy," he said. "You may not be a bucket of brains, but you're fast and you have sharp teeth. Sometimes that's all a rat needs to get the job done."

"Gee, thanks, Boss," said Scurvy, stunned by the compliment.

Dupont turned to Glory and her father, who stood before him, their paws manacled together.

"Two for the price of one!" exulted the rat leader. "This is better than I could have hoped for." He cocked his large gray head, regarding them with relish. "Doesn't this make a pretty picture!" he crowed. "Like father, like daughter. You Goldenleafs thought you'd given me the slip, didn't you?"

Neither mouse said a word. Dupont swaggered closer.

"I said, you thought you'd given me the slip!" He thrust his snout first into Glory's face, and then into her father's. "Me, Roquefort Dupont, ruler of thousands! Me, Roquefort Dupont, Lord of the Sewers and supreme leader of the rat realm! Me, Roquefort Dupont, descendant of kings!" He strutted across the gloomy chamber, gloating.

"You've descended all right," Glory said scornfully. She surveyed the smelly, trash-strewn hole that served as Dupont's headquarters with disdain. "It doesn't get much lower than this."

"Insolence!" screamed Dupont, launching himself toward her. "I'll have your ears for that!"

Behind him, Scurvy quailed, but Glory held her ground. Dupont stopped just inches from where she stood.

"Look down your nose at me, will you?" Dupont snarled, his face so close to hers that Glory could smell the anchovy on his breath. "It's high time someone showed you just how insignificant you are."

Glory's temper surged. She leaned toward Dupont until her elegant little nose was pressed right up against his hideous snout. "I hate to be the one to have to tell you this, your royal thugness," she said. "But you need a breath mint."

Scurvy's eyes popped at this. No one talked to the boss like that and lived to tell the tale!

Dupont drew back. His tail thrashed. His red eyes narrowed. He reached out with one paw and hooked a single sharp claw beneath Glory's chin. She held his gaze unflinchingly.

"I loathe everything about mice," he said softly. "The way you look, the way you smell, the way you think you're so superior, what with your books and your libraries and your ridiculous guilds. You'd almost think you were trying to be human!" Dupont's voice grew louder as he warmed to his theme. "You mice give rodents a bad name. You don't deserve to have tails! And maybe that's a good thing, because I'm only too happy to relieve you of them." A menacing smile crept across the large rat's face. "As I always say, the only good mouse is a dead mouse. You and your kind have exploited us rats for centuries, shoving us away in the darkest corners and keeping us from our rightful place above ground. We should be the ones in charge, not you! Well, all that is about to change. The reign of mice is over in this city as of tomorrow night! That's right, tomorrow night! All thanks to me, Roquefort Dupont!"

There was a hint of madness in the rat's eyes, which gleamed red as twin flames in the gloom. He smirked at Glory. "Tomorrow night, you mice are history," he continued. "But for you and your father, it ends right here and now." Dupont placed his hairy snout next to Glory's elegant little ear. "Did you happen to notice my collection?" he whispered. "All it needs is that charming little tail of yours to make it complete. Oh, and your ears as well, of course. Mousemeat, Glory Goldenleaf. You are going to be mousemeat."

Glory's bright little eyes flicked ever so briefly over the gray rat's shoulder to the wall of horrors beyond. Her heart was thumping wildly. Fear and terror were Dupont's tactics, her father had said. And what was her weapon against them? *Courage.* Mustering every ounce of determination in her little body, she held her ground.

"Think you're brave, do you?" Dupont sneered. "They all think they're brave, until they get a taste of my bite." He snapped his razor-sharp teeth together and laughed. "It's infinitely worse than my bark, I assure you."

"You're a monster," said Glory in a low voice.

"What was that?" asked Dupont, looking pleased. He cocked a large gray ear in her direction with a dramatic flourish. "A monster, you say?" He puffed out his chest slightly and preened. "Why, thank you, Miss Goldenleaf,

I take that as quite a compliment."

Dupont began to pace again. "In fact, now that you mention it, I find I'm suddenly struck with a *monstrously* good idea!" he exclaimed. "Oh, yes, a most fiendishly wonderful idea!" He cast a shrewd glance at Glory and her father. "The two of you have caused me a great deal of trouble, and as a consequence I think you deserve a great deal more pain in return. And so, before I add your, ah, *extremities* to my collection, I think perhaps I'll wrap you both up and deliver you back to the Spy Museum instead. A most timely present, just in time for the EXTERMINATOR!"

Dupont's voice rose to a triumphant shriek, and Limburger Lulu and Limburger Louie began skipping around the chamber, chanting, "Exterminate! Exterminate! Put an End to Short Tails!"

"Shut up, you fools!" snapped Dupont.

The twin rats-in-waiting fell instantly silent.

"Scurvy!"

Dupont's aide snapped to attention. "Yes, Boss?"

"Return the prisoners to the cage, then go find Gnaw and report back here on the double. It's time to start the countdown to Operation P.E.S.T. Control."

CHAPTER 19

DAY TWO—
SATURDAY
1715 HOURS

Oz pressed his ear to the knothole of the towering tree just inside the gates to Dumbarton Oaks. Somewhere deep inside, he could hear the faint sound of music. Rock music.

"This must be it," he said.

Bunsen popped his head out of Oz's shirt pocket. "Let me have a listen," he said.

Oz held out his hand and Bunsen climbed on, gripping Oz's thumb tightly as the boy lifted him closer to the tree. He cocked one pale ear toward the knothole. "Definitely the right place," he said, wincing. "There's no mistaking the, uh, *robust* sound of the Steel Acorns."

Oz placed Bunsen back in his pocket and put his mouth to the knothole. "B-Nut, if you're in there, Glory's in trouble!" he called.

He stood back and waited. Nothing.

"Try again," said D. B. "Only louder this time."

"Much louder," added Bunsen, "if you want to be heard above that racket."

"B-NUT! GLORY'S IN TROUBLE!" Oz yelled, but again there was no reply.

"I can't believe he didn't hear you that time," said D. B.

"Maybe we have the wrong tree," said Oz doubtfully, scanning the estate grounds for a likelier candidate.

"I heard you just fine."

Oz whirled around to see a nose emerge from the knothole. A nose remarkably similar to Glory's.

"B-Nut?" asked Oz.

Glory's brother eyed him cautiously. Bunsen poked his head out of Oz's pocket. "It all right, B-Nut," he said. "They're friends of Glory's."

"Friends of Glory's?" B-Nut looked astounded. "My sister broke the Mouse Code? She really must be in trouble."

"It's a long story," said Bunsen, "and we haven't much time."

"What's up?"

As Oz started to explain what had happened back at Dupont Circle, B-Nut's whiskers twitched in alarm. "Glory went into his *lair*? Without *backup*?"

"There's more," said Bunsen. "She got the Kiss of Death back, but then she went in again." He hesitated. "B-Nut, she found your father."

B-Nut's whiskers trembled. "My father?"

Oz nodded. "He's still alive. Dupont has him in a cage."

"And then something went wrong—" added D. B.

"We tried to reel them in, but—"

"The fishing line was cut, and—"

B-Nut's head swiveled from D. B. to Oz to Bunsen and back again as they all rushed to tell him what had happened. Finally, he held up a paw. "Hold on a minute. You're all talking at once. Bunsen, you explain."

Briskly, the lab mouse outlined the afternoon's events, starting with Glory's e-mail to him and ending with her capture.

"I see," B-Nut said when Bunsen had finished. "She certainly has moxie, my sister. Took photos of Dupont's lair, you say? And planted a transmitter?" He shook his head in admiration. "Well, there's no time to be lost. We have to go in after them."

"Don't you think we should alert the Mouse Guard?" said Bunsen. "Or Julius?"

B-Nut frowned. "It would take them hours to mount a rescue. We can be back at the Metro station in two shakes of a rat's tail. Besides, I've learned a thing or two about Dupont and his famous rat kingdom on my surveillance runs. I think I know just the thing to rattle his cage. But we're going to need more help."

Poking his head back into the knothole, he gave a sharp whistle.

A minute later, three more small heads popped out. Three pairs of bright little mouse eyes widened in alarm at the sight of Oz and D. B.

"Dude!" said a dark gray mouse who had slicked the fur on top of his head into sharp spikes. "Are you talking to humans?"

"It's cool, Tulip," said B-Nut. "They're friends of Glory's."

His band mate frowned. "It's just Lip, dude, remember? I hate it when you call me Tulip."

"Right," said B-Nut. "Sorry, Lip. Oz, D. B., Bunsen, meet the Steel Acorns. This is Lip—he's lead guitar. Romeo plays bass, and Nutmeg's our drummer."

The band members waved shyly. Oz and D. B. waved back.

"Lip, you and the guys grab our gear and catch a pigeon to Dupont Circle," said B-Nut. "Oh, and bring my skateboard. I'm going to go with Bunsen and the humans—"

"We've got a gig at Dupont Circle?" Lip looked confused.

B-Nut sighed. "Just bring the gear, dude. I'll explain everything when we get there. And hurry, there are lives at stake."

"Oh, I get it, spy stuff. Awesome!"

The Steel Acorns vanished, and Oz held out his hand. B-Nut hesitated for a moment, then hopped onto his palm.

"Closest I've been to a human before," said B-Nut, giving Oz a tentative sniff. "You don't smell all that bad."

"Thanks," said Oz doubtfully. "I guess."

The rendezvous at Dupont Circle went off without a hitch. Lip, Romeo, and Nutmeg were waiting for them under one of the chess tables at the park, and after stowing the Steel Acorns and their gear into shirt and jacket pockets, Oz and D. B. headed for the escalator to the Metro station.

"So what's your plan, B-Nut?" Oz asked as they approached the bench that concealed the entrance to Dupont's lair.

B-Nut poked his head out of Oz's shirt pocket and gave him a cocky grin. "You'll see," he replied. "Bunsen, is that dog-doo transmitter Glory took in with her still in place?"

Bunsen poked Oz with his paw. Oz held up his CD player and the lab mouse hopped onto it. He fiddled with the dial, tuning it in to the transmitter's frequency. Then he and B-Nut stationed themselves by the headphones and listened closely.

"It's past my DINNERTIME!" Roquefort Dupont's unmistakable voice came booming through loud and clear. "Where are those worthless rats-in-waiting?"

B-Nut clapped Bunsen on the back. "Nice work, Bunsen."

"Thanks," said Bunsen, slightly puzzled. "Though I don't see how eavesdropping on Dupont is going to help Glory."

"Actually," said B-Nut, "I was hoping we could reverse the feed and let the rats do a little eavesdropping on us instead."

Bunsen's pink eyes widened. "Ah," he said. "I think I catch your drift. Very clever."

"What can we do to help?" asked Oz.

"Keep an eye out for rats," said B-Nut. "Oh, and here." He passed his skateboard to Oz. "Glory's should be around here somewhere, too, right? See if you can tie them together. A rubber band should do the trick. Then secure them both to the fishing line."

"Check," said Oz.

As B-Nut and Bunsen busied themselves loading a backpack with supplies, Lip and Romeo and Nutmeg plugged their electric guitars (made from tongue depressors wired for sound by a second cousin of Bunsen's) into the amplifiers (Mouse Music's finest, crafted from foraged hearing aids).

"Time to suit up, Bunsen, we're going in," said B-Nut, strapping the backpack on.

"Me?" squeaked Bunsen in alarm.

"Can't play the guitar, can you?"

The slim white mouse shook his head. "Well, no, I—"

"Then you're it, dude! I can't go in without backup."

"But I'm a lab mouse!"

B-Nut slapped him on the shoulder. "Sure, dude. One heck of a lab mouse. Look like you're in good shape, too. Been working out?"

"I, uh—"

"Thought so. Quiet lab mouse is just your cover, isn't it? There's more to old Bunsen than meets the eye. It'll be a cinch—just follow my lead."

Jamming his helmet on, B-Nut stuffed a small wad of cotton in each ear. He handed some to Bunsen and instructed him to do the same. Reluctantly, Bunsen did as he was told. B-Nut placed a helmet on his colleague's head and gave him a once-over. "You are so pale, dude," he said. "You could use some camouflage. The rats will spot you a mile away."

"I told you, I'm a lab mouse," said Bunsen sadly, glancing down at his white fur. Then he brightened. "Maybe I have something that will help." He rummaged in his duffel bag and emerged a moment later with a small tin of black shoe polish.

"Bunsen, you think of everything!" said B-Nut.

"One does one's best," Bunsen replied modestly.

While D. B. helped Bunsen swipe shoe polish onto his pale coat and tail, B-Nut made the final preparations.

"Skateboards ready?" he called to Oz.

Oz gave him a thumbs-up.

"Acorns ready?"

Lip played a quick riff on his guitar in reply.

"Good luck," said Oz. "I wish we could go in there with you."

B-Nut grinned at him. "Sorry, kid. This is a job for a mouse." He turned to Bunsen, who now resembled a small black mole. "That's more like it, dude. You look like a real commando. Okay, Acorns, it's time to rock and roll!"

Bunsen flipped a switch on Oz's CD player and turned the volume up to maximum. As the Acorns lit into their number-one hit ("Born to Shake My Tail"), B-Nut leaped onto the lead skateboard. Bunsen climbed cautiously onto the one in the rear and sat down, gripping his paws around the edges for dear life.

"Remember, three tugs on the line when we're ready for you to pull us up," said B-Nut.

"You got it," Oz replied.

With a powerful thrust of his hind paw, B-Nut pushed off and sped toward the hole beneath the bench, whisking Bunsen—pink eyes squeezed tightly shut—along behind him like the caboose on a train.

As the tiny rescue party vanished from sight, Oz shook his head in concern. "I hope this works," he said to D. B. "I just hope this works."

CHAPTER 20

DAY TWO—
SATURDAY
1800 HOURS

"EeeeeeeeeOWWWWWW!"

Dupont shrieked as a deafening blast of hard-driving rock music pierced the air of his headquarters. Scurvy and Gnaw squealed and dived for cover, their paws clamped firmly over their ears (Gnaw covered just one). Limburger Lulu and her brother fled down the corridor toward the sewer, squeaking in terror.

"WHAT IS THAT RACKET?!" screeched Dupont.

No one answered. His aides were too busy rolling themselves into tight little balls of gray fur in a futile attempt to avoid the high-pitched whine of the electric guitars. The music pulsed and throbbed and split the air. It seemed to be coming from all directions.

Back in their cage in the shadows, Glory and her

father had their paws clamped over their ears too. After a minute, though, Glory nudged her father.

"Pop," she whispered. "Pop, that's the Steel Acorns."

Dumbarton Goldenleaf cautiously lifted one paw away from one dignified ear. "I do believe you're right," he said, listening intently. "'Born to Shake My Tail,' if I'm not mistaken."

"You're not mistaken. It's B-Nut!" said Glory. "He's come for us!"

Her father smiled. "Clever boy," he said. "Rat ears are highly sensitive—much more so than ours. Dupont and his cronies must be going berserk."

Indeed they were, to judge from the thrashing and howling that could be heard through the raucous wails of the Acorns' guitars.

Glory stood up and helped her father to his feet. "We have to be ready for him," she said. "B-Nut will be moving fast."

Indeed he was—and so was Bunsen. Still gripping the edges of Glory's skateboard grimly in his blackened paws, Bunsen shot through the tunnel and into Dupont's lair right behind B-Nut. The two mice landed in a heap atop a crumpled brown paper lunch bag. Fortunately, they arrived unobserved, as every rat eye in the chamber was squeezed tightly shut in a vain attempt to help block out the earsplitting music.

B-Nut hopped off his skateboard and gave Bunsen an enthusiastic grin. Bunsen, looking dazed, managed a weak smile in return. The two mice grabbed their skateboards—still linked together with a rubber band—and scuttled for cover behind the lunch bag. B-Nut peered around it just as a fresh wave of feedback screeched from the dog-doo transmitter.

"OWWWWWWWW!!! MAKE IT STOP!!!" wailed Dupont, but for once neither Gnaw nor Scurvy, who still lay prone on the floor, rushed to do his bidding.

B-Nut opened his backpack and removed what appeared to be a pen. Hefting it onto his shoulder, he aimed it toward the middle of the chamber and pressed down on the clip. Instantly, a misty stream of liquid jetted out toward the rats. B-Nut ducked back down again and Bunsen passed him a gas mask (crafted from bits of an old rubber glove stuffed with cheesecloth), then hastily pulled on his own. A thick haze of homemade tear gas (juice from foraged onions) began to fill the chamber.

"IT'S—A—RAID!" Dupont managed to choke out before he sagged to the floor by his aides. The three of them lay there, gasping for breath and weeping uncontrollably. Roquefort Dupont, descendant of kings, Lord of the Sewers and supreme ruler of Washington's rat underworld, was powerless. He could do nothing but swipe his tail at B-Nut and Bunsen in feeble anger as the two mice leaped over the lunch bag and sped across the room toward the far corner.

In a trice they reached the cage and wrenched open the door. B-Nut swiftly removed the handcuffs from his father and sister. He flung his father—who was also overcome by the onion juice—over his shoulder and motioned to Bunsen to grab Glory. Dupont watched in helpless rage as the rescue party secured their charges and then sat down behind them on the skateboards.

"*Just—you—wait!*" he sobbed, wiping at his stream-ing red eyes. "*It's—not—over—yet!*"

The mice ignored him. B-Nut gave three sharp tugs on the fishing line, and the skateboards shot forward into the darkness of the tunnel.

CHAPTER 21

DAY TWO—
SATURDAY
1830 HOURS

The doors to Central Command flew open as Glory burst into the Spy Mice Agency headquarters. She was breathless and disheveled, her normally glossy and impeccably groomed brown fur streaked with dust and bits of garbage.

"Julius!" she cried.

Her boss, who was deep in conversation with Fumble, looked up in surprise. He frowned.

"Julius, you're never going to believe—"

The elder mouse held up a paw, silencing her. "Glory, tell me the truth," he said sternly, crossing the room toward her. "Did you break the Mouse Code? Fumble here tells me he saw you speaking to two children this afternoon."

Fumble was trying to appear regretful at having to

be the one to impart this distressing information, but he was failing miserably. A smug smile crept across his broad gray face. Glory shot him a poisonous glance. She turned back to Julius. "Yes, but—"

"And unauthorized use of Agency property? Is this also true?"

"Yes, but—"

"Did Bunsen provide you with equipment from Deep Freeze?"

"Yes, but—"

"I'm sorry, Glory, there are no buts about it. This is a serious breach of protocol. Outright insubordination, in fact."

"Julius, please give me a chance to explain!" Glory implored. "My pigeon taxi got me here just as fast as he could! The others are on their way. You see, the rats—"

The Spy Mice Agency director cut her off. "Excuses are pointless," he said. "I'm afraid I'm going to have to call in the Mouse Guard. You're under arrest, Glory."

Glory's shoulders sagged. Her elegant little ears drooped. She glared at Fumble, who was now grinning broadly. Odious great toadying lump! This was all his fault! Hot tears of anger and frustration welled up in Glory's bright little eyes.

The doors to Central Command burst open again

with a loud bang. Julius flinched and snapped, "Haven't I told you mice not to—"

"Well, if it isn't Julius Folger, as I live and breathe."

Julius whirled around. Dumbarton Goldenleaf stood in the doorway. The Spy Mice Agency director's mouth dropped open. Glory's father saluted him and winked at Glory. "Sorry, sweetheart," he said to her. "B-Nut and I got stuck on a trainee pigeon, of all the worse luck, and ended up halfway to the White House. We had to practically draw the birdbrain a map to get here."

"General Goldenleaf!" Julius was astounded.

"The very same—well, almost." Glory's father glanced ruefully at the stub of his once-proud tail.

"But Dumbarton, I thought—we all thought—"

"That I was dead? Naturally, as would have I. But Dupont decided that I might prove of use as a bargaining chip eventually and that it was worth his while to keep me alive. If you can call being stuck in a cage for three months with nothing but disgusting rat leftovers *living*." Glory's father shuddered.

"How did you—"

"Escape? I didn't. My brave children rescued me."

"Oh my," said Julius faintly.

B-Nut pushed past his father into the room. He held

the Kiss of Death in his paws. "Glory got this back for you," he announced, laying it at Julius's feet.

"And," said Bunsen, who was right behind him, "she also managed to photograph Rat HQ. Not to mention plant a homing device on Dupont." He handed the watch camera to Julius and smiled shyly at Glory.

"Did she, indeed?" murmured Julius. He glanced at the slim lab mouse and did a double take. "Bunsen? Is that you? What on earth are you doing covered in shoe polish?"

Glory stepped forward and took Bunsen by the paw. A close observer might have detected the faint tinge of pink that appeared beneath the lab mouse's disguise. "Bunsen was the brains behind the rescue mission."

"Not to mention much of the brawn," added B-Nut. "He came with me when I went into Dupont's lair after these two."

Behind Julius, the smug smile began to falter on Fumble's face. Julius looked at the mice who stood before him. "It appears I may have been a bit hasty," he said.

A tendril of hope sprouted in Glory's heart. "You mean I'm not under arrest?"

The elder mouse shook his head. "No, my dear, you are most definitely not under arrest. And I most humbly apologize for mistrusting you. Your ingenuity and pluck are an example to us all. I only wish all my staff were so clever." He shot a troubled glance at Fumble, who by now was squirming visibly. Julius placed his paw on Glory's shoulder, being careful to avoid the bandage. "Glory Goldenleaf," he intoned solemnly, "I hereby fully reinstate you as a field agent for the Spy Mice Agency. And not only that, but I also promote you to Silver Skateboard."

Glory's heart soared. Silver Skateboard! This was better than she could have ever dreamed! Her boss extended his paw and she shook it heartily, aiming a triumphant glance at Fumble. Her house mouse colleague began to back toward the door.

"Hey, you forgot to say anything about us!" said Lip, nearly knocking him down as he bounced in. The other two band members were close on his tail.

B-Nut grinned. "Julius Folger, meet the Steel Acorns. Tulip—I mean Lip—Romeo, and Nutmeg. Your newest recruits. Secret agents by day, rock band by night."

"You don't say," said Julius in surprise. "Well, that's certainly an original cover." He turned back to Glory. "Now, what is all this about humans?"

As Glory explained the part that Oz and D. B. had played in the retrieval and rescue mission, Julius just kept shaking his head.

"I think it's best that the Council knows nothing of this," he said when she was finished. "It will just have to be our little Agency secret. And yours too, of course, Dumbarton, if you agree."

"For your paws only," promised Glory's father.

Julius placed his right paw over his heart. "All together now, word of honor as mice," he said.

"Word of honor," the mice replied solemnly, placing their paws over their hearts.

"Fumble, that means you as well," said Julius sharply.

Fumble, who was still trying to make an exit unseen, halted. He nodded reluctantly and lifted his paw to his chest.

"And I trust that you had only the highest intentions today in informing on Glory and Bunsen," Julius added. "I will not stand for tattletales or backstabbers on my staff."

"No, sir. I mean yes, sir," muttered Fumble, and slunk dejectedly from the room.

"There's just one more thing," said Bunsen. "Do you recall the fake plastic dog-doo transmitter?"

"How could I forget it?" Julius replied, a trace of sarcasm in his voice. "The very pinnacle of human ingenuity."

Bunsen crossed to the main receiver and fiddled with the controls, adjusting the frequency. Suddenly, Dupont's voice filled Central Command.

"Those mice think they can pull the wool over my eyes! Me, Roquefort Dupont, descendant of kings! Well, they've got another think coming. In just a few hours, when we launch Operation P.E.S.T. Control, their little tails will be mine! MINE, I tell you!"

"Operation P.E.S.T. Control?" said Julius.

"Put an End to Short Tails," Glory explained.

"We'll just see about that," Julius replied softly. "Operation P.E.S.T. Control, is it? We'll just see who's the pest around here, Mr. Roquefort High-and-Mighty-Dupont, and just who's in control."

He turned to Bunsen. "Was this your idea, Mr. Burner? Planting a bug at Rat HQ?"

Bunsen swallowed nervously and nodded. "I thought perhaps the rats, being, well, rats and all, might just overlook a pile of, um, dog doo."

"The watch-camera was his idea, too," added Glory. "And the homing device."

"We'll be able to track Dupont's movements with it, sir," said the lab mouse.

Julius smiled. He clapped Bunsen on the shoulder. "Well done, young mouse, well done. I'm beginning to think there's more to you than meets the eye. B-Nut, Glory, effective immediately Bunsen will be joining your ranks as a field agent."

Bunsen blushed again, and darted a glance at Glory, who smiled broadly at him in return. "Bunsen, you are true blue," she said.

"And now," said Julius. "I do believe it's time I met the children."

CHAPTER 22

DAY THREE—
SUNDAY
1730 HOURS

"I do not believe I have to do this," said D. B. "I do not believe I have to be the back end of a horse."

Oz gave a snort of laughter. "Well, actually, it's a donkey, not a horse," he replied. "I'd trade places with you if I could, but you're too short to see out the eyeholes."

Oz's phone call to Australia had worked. Somehow, his mother had talked the opera company's wardrobe manager into loaning them a costume. Not a horse costume, unfortunately, but almost as good. The large box had arrived at Oz's house from the National Opera just a few minutes ago.

"Oh, so now you're telling me we're going to the Halloween party as the Trojan Donkey, not the Trojan Horse?" D. B.'s voice was somewhat muffled by the heavy gray fabric. "That's the stupidest thing I ever heard."

"No one will know the difference," Oz consoled her. "But I'll pin a sign on us just in case."

A deep sigh emerged from the costume's rear end. "A sign? Our costume is so dumb we have to wear a sign to explain it? How lame is that?"

Oz's father poked his head into the living room.

"Almost ready, my little sugarplums?" he said. "We have to leave soon, or I'll be late." He caught sight of the costume and raised his bushy eyebrows. "The Trojan Horse! Very clever. I'm sure you'll win a prize."

"See? The costume's not so lame—my dad knew who we were right away," Oz whispered as his father left the room again.

"Maybe you're right," D. B. replied reluctantly, wriggling her way out of the donkey's hindquarters as Oz carefully removed the heavy gray wire-and-fabric head. "But do you really think this will work?"

"It'll work," said Oz. "Glory said so, remember?"

As the two of them bundled the costume back into the box, Oz noticed an envelope in the bottom. He picked it up and opened it. There was a single sheet of white paper inside on which were printed the words: IT AIN'T OVER . . .

Oz smiled. "Until the fat lady sings," he finished in

a whisper. It was a message from his mother in their own private code. A silly little saying left over from babyhood. *Thanks, Mom,* he thought to himself. *I love you too.*

"What's that about?" asked D. B., glancing curiously over his shoulder.

"Nothing—just a note from my mom." Oz folded the paper back into the envelope and stuck it in the pocket of his jeans. For good luck.

"Have you got the other stuff? The stuff Bunsen told us to bring?"

Oz nodded, holding up his Chester B. Arthur Elementary gym bag. Inside was his father's fishing net and a flashlight. He placed the bag in the box on top of the costume, and then he and D. B. carried the box outside to the curb.

"Are you sure your mother and her camera crew are going to be there tonight?" asked Oz as they waited for his father.

"I'm sure," said D. B. "She said this party's the hottest ticket in all of Washington, and that she wouldn't miss it for the world."

Luigi Levinson appeared on the doorstep. He had on blue knee breeches and a matching jacket, a white ruffled shirt, and a white wig.

"Let me guess—George Washington," said D. B.

Oz's father struck a presidential pose. "I cannot tell a lie," he said. "I am indeed."

"I didn't know old Wooden Teeth was a spy," D. B. said to Oz as they wedged their costume box into the trunk.

Oz nodded. "Spymaster, actually. He ran a ring of spies during the Revolutionary War."

A few minutes later, they pulled up in front of the Spy Museum.

"Will you two be all right on your own?" Oz's father asked. "I've got to help the caterers."

"Sure, Dad," said Oz.

"You can change in the conference room upstairs," his father added. "Just don't touch anything."

D. B. was silent as she and Oz wrestled the box into the employee elevator.

"You're not really mad that you have to be the back end of the horse, are you?" asked Oz, pressing the button for the fourth floor.

"Donkey," corrected D. B.

"Okay, then, donkey."

D. B. shook her head. "Nah. I'm just worried about Glory and Bunsen and the others, that's all. I'd hate for anything to happen to them."

"Yeah, I know what you mean," Oz agreed.

He thought back to their brief meeting with Julius in the hallway behind the café after yesterday's rescue operation. As Glory had made the introductions, the elder mouse had stepped right onto his palm and looked him fearlessly in the eye.

"So you are Ozymandias," he'd said.

"Just Oz," Oz had replied.

"Just Oz, is it?" the Spy Mice Agency director had peered at him intently. "Never be ashamed of who you are, young man. It's a fine name, from a fine poem. *'I met a traveller from an antique land'*—Percy Bysshe Shelley at his best. It's a name any mouse would be proud to call his own, and you should be proud of it too."

Before Oz could reply, Julius had continued, "We mice owe you and Miss Delilah here a great debt of thanks, it would seem. And I understand Glory has made arrangements to repay at least part of it tomorrow night."

Bunsen and Glory had taken over after that, outlining their plan for foiling Dupont's attack and settling Oz and D. B.'s score with Jordan Scott and Tank Wilson. Now, thought Oz, as he and D. B. slid the box off the elevator and down the corridor to the conference room, he wondered if what had seemed brilliant yesterday was such a good idea after all. Were the mice having second thoughts too?

D. B. looked at her watch. "The rendezvous is set for 6:45," she said. "I mean 1845 hours. That doesn't give us much time. We'd better head for Checkpoint Charlie before we stuff ourselves into this rig."

Oz nodded and pulled the flashlight from his gym bag. After a quick look around to make sure nobody was watching, the two of them headed down the employee staircase. They emerged near the Fly, Spy! exhibit in total darkness. The museum was deserted, the exhibits closed for the night. It was eerily quiet.

"This is creepy," said D. B.

Oz nodded in agreement. The mice had insisted on changing the location of the dead drop because, as Glory had explained, "the hallway behind the café will be crawling with caterers."

Keeping a sharp lookout for security guards, Oz and D. B. followed the flashlight's narrow beam down the empty corridors and through the silent exhibits. They crept past the Library and tiptoed through Sisterhood of Spies on to the World War II–era exhibits. Shadows loomed around the fake French farmhouse where resistance fighters had hidden from the Nazis. They skirted the D-day army jeep, and the hair on the back of Oz's neck lifted when D. B. reached out and grabbed his polo shirt.

"Jeez, D. B.," he gasped. "Scare me to death, why don't you."

"Sorry."

They flew down the stairs to the rooms decked out as East and West Germany during the cold war and crept along the phony sandbagged Berlin Wall to Checkpoint Charlie.

"There it is," whispered Oz, pointing his flashlight across an exhibit set up to look like a 1950s-era German café.

A shabby, old-fashioned telephone booth stood against the far wall. During the day, museumgoers could lift the handset and listen to the story of a pair of married double agents. No time for that now. Oz opened the phone booth door. It creaked loudly and D. B. jumped, nearly toppling him.

"Sorry," she whispered again.

"Hey! Who's there!" A loud voice shattered the silence.

Oz and D. B. leaped into the telephone booth.

"Oof," said D. B. There was barely room for one person inside, let alone one plus Oz.

"Sorry." Oz squeezed the door shut behind them and switched off the flashlight.

The two of them crouched in the darkness, hardly daring to breathe. The heavy tread of footsteps heralded a security guard's approach.

"Is anyone there? Herbie, if you're playing a trick on me again, I will have your badge for breakfast."

The security guard stood there for a minute, playing his flashlight over the furniture and walls. Seeing and hearing nothing, he grunted and moved on. Oz and D. B. waited a bit to be sure he didn't double back, then opened the phone booth door and tumbled out onto the floor.

"Hurry up," said D. B. crossly. "I've had enough of this place."

Oz pointed the flashlight under the wooden slat that served as the booth's bench. Sure enough, there was the package that Bunsen had promised would be left for them. The mice had taped it to the bottom of the bench.

"Let's get out of here," he said, grabbing it, and led the way back upstairs.

Back in the conference room, Oz placed the package (neatly wrapped in newspaper and tied with foraged string) on the table. He opened it. Inside were Oz's CD player, some headphones for D. B. and what looked like a small, 1960s-era transistor radio. D. B. sighed. "Just like my grandfather's," she said. "I should have known."

"I'm sure it'll work just fine," said Oz, plugging his headphones into his newly Bunsenized CD player. D. B. put her headphones on as well.

"Hello? Hello? Anyone there?" said Oz. "Testing, one, two, three, four, testing."

"Houston, we have liftoff!" replied a voice. A familiar voice.

"Bunsen!" cried Oz. He could hear squeaks and cheers from the other mice in the background. "You're coming through loud and clear."

"So are you, Oz," said Bunsen. "How about you, D. B., are you there as well?"

"Right here."

"Okay. I've got you both wired into Central Command here and to Glory and B-Nut as well. Say hello, Goldenleafs."

"Hi, kids!" B-Nut replied.

"Strap on your helmets, mouselings, we're in for a wild ride," added Glory.

"General Goldenleaf and the Mouse Guard are moving into position as we speak," the lab mouse continued. "They'll be monitoring our transmissions throughout the evening and are fully prepared to step in if anything goes wrong. Now that we're sure all the equipment is operational, I'm going to switch us all to standby mode. If you need anything, just tap your volume control button twice. Otherwise, we'll rendezvous at 1845 hours as planned."

"Roger," said Oz. "Over and out."

He turned to D. B. and grinned. "The name is Levinson, Oz Levinson," he said.

D. B. rolled her eyes and reached for the donkey's hindquarters. "Get a move on, secret agent boy," she said, stepping into the costume. "It's time to go undercover."

CHAPTER 23

DAY THREE—
SUNDAY
1845 HOURS

Oz and D. B. stood on the sidewalk outside the front entrance to the Spy Museum. It was a beautiful night. Stars glittered in the dark sky above, and a harvest moon beamed down on them like a huge Halloween pumpkin. Despite the late October chill, it was hot inside the costume, and the gray fabric itched. The wire framework that held the donkey's head up rested heavily on Oz's shoulders, and he shifted uncomfortably.

"Stop wiggling, Oz." It was Glory, her voice transmitting clear as a bell through Oz's headphones. "I'm coming in for a landing."

Oz peered out through the costume's eyeholes. Above him, a pigeon circled lazily in the air. Beneath the bird he spotted a small white dinner-napkin parachute floating down toward him. Glory was suspended from it. She waved.

A few seconds later Oz heard a tiny thump as she landed on the costume's head.

"Agent in place," she reported.

"Agents in place here too," Oz added. He couldn't suppress a grin. He was beginning to feel like a real secret agent. "The name is Levinson, Oz Levinson," he murmured again under his breath. "World-famous boy spy."

"Well done, everyone," said Julius. "Right on schedule. I'm handing the reins over to Mr. Burner."

Oz heard the lab mouse clear his throat. "Fifteen minutes to showtime," Bunsen said. "The Mouse Guard has been deployed, and B-Nut and Hank are in position. Just exactly where are you, B-Nut?"

"Circling between the Metro Center and Gallery Place stations. No sign of Dupont yet from either."

"He's definitely on his way," Bunsen replied. "The computer gymnasts are up on the administrative floor, tracking his homing signal on the museum director's computer. They just relayed an update. He's only a few blocks away."

Oz pressed his face against the eyeholes of his costume again and carefully scanned the street in front of him. There was no sign of the Mouse Guard, but he knew they were there, hidden in the shadows that draped the curbs and softened the sharp edges of the buildings along on Ninth and F Streets. The mice's last line of defense if tonight's plan somehow went wrong. And if it did, Oz wondered, would General Goldenleaf and his warriors be enough to hold back Roquefort Dupont and his forces?

A limousine pulled up and a woman dressed in a black leather jumpsuit got out. Oz recognized her costume instantly; he'd seen pictures of it hanging upstairs in the Spy Games exhibit.

"Agent Emma Peel from that old 1960s TV show," Oz reported to the back end of the Trojan Horse.

"What TV show?" snapped D. B., who was growing cranky because she couldn't see anything.

"*The Avengers.* Ask your mother, she'll remember it."

"Oh look, Jeffrey, the Trojan Horse!" said the Emma Peel to her escort, who in his white dinner jacket and black bowtie was clearly meant to be James Bond. Although Oz couldn't remember ever seeing a bald James Bond before. "Isn't that charming."

"Charming?" retorted D. B.

"Hey, at least they didn't notice we're actually a donkey," Oz whispered back.

A steady stream of limousines and taxis began to form a line in front of the museum entrance. Oz kept up a running commentary so D. B. wouldn't feel left out.

"Okay, let's see, here comes—oh, gee, that's Senator What's-his-name, from California, the one who used to be a movie star. He's dressed as Julius Caesar. Did you know Caesar invented codes? Behind him is some guy with a raven on his shoulder—oh, I know, he's supposed to be Edgar Allan Poe. He was a master code breaker. And two more James Bonds, and a guy talking into his shoe— hey, it's the president's National Security Advisor!"

"A guy talking into his shoe advises the president?" D. B. sounded indignant. "Couldn't they find anyone better than that?"

"It's part of the costume, you goof. He doesn't do that in real life. He's dressed as Maxwell Smart. From another one of those '60 shows."

"I give up," said D. B. "How do you know all this stuff?"

Oz shrugged, which set the donkey head rocking back and forth. "I spend a lot of time here, remember?"

"Guess I've still got a lot to learn about espionage," said D. B.

Just then, the Chester B. Arthur Elementary school bus pulled up, along with the Channel 12 news van.

"Your mom's here with her camera crew!" Oz said. "And so's our class."

He and D. B. stood very still as the fifth and sixth graders got off the bus and filed past. Their schoolmates were in high spirits, laughing and jostling one another as they pushed into the building. Some of the girls wore glasses and carried notebooks ("Harriet the Spies galore," whispered Oz), and there were a lot of trenchcoats and dark glasses.

"Hi, sweetie!" said D. B.'s mom, aiming a pat at the costume's rump. "Don't you two look adorable."

"Mo-om!" D. B. wailed. "We're not supposed to look *adorable*. We are the Trojan Horse! We are full of fierce warriors. Go away!"

Amelia Bean gave the back end of the donkey another pat and moved off toward the National Security Advisor. Her camera crew, busy panning the illustrious crowd, followed.

"What's Mrs. Busby wearing?" asked D. B., once she was gone.

"Um, she's got something wrapped around her head," whispered Oz. "I think she's Harriet Tubman."

"She spied for the Union army during the Civil War when she led slaves to freedom, right?" said D. B. "That much I do know. How about Jordan and Tank?"

Oz squinted through the costume's eyeholes. There they were, the last stragglers off the bus. "I see Tank," he reported. "What a moron! He didn't even bother to wear a costume. No, wait, I'm wrong. He—"

"He what?" D. B. demanded.

Oz snorted in disbelief. Tank had what looked like gold foil wrapped around the index finger of his right hand. "And you thought putting a Trojan Horse sign on our costume was lame," he said. "Wait till you get a load of this."

"What? What's he wearing?" D. B. demanded again.

"He's got gold wrapping paper on his finger. Get it? Goldfinger? You know, the bad guy from the Bond movies?"

D. B. groaned. "Definitely lame," she agreed. "How about Jordan?"

Oz looked over at Jordan Scott. His heart sank. Sometimes life was so unfair. Jordan was dressed exactly how he, Oz Levinson, future secret agent, would have dressed for the masquerade party if he hadn't been stuck in a stupid donkey suit. His classmate wore a black tuxedo, white dress shirt, and black bow tie. There was a red carnation in his lapel. His hair was slicked back, and he had a smug smile on his face. He didn't look twice at the Trojan Horse as he sauntered past into the museum.

"Well?" D. B. was getting impatient.

Oz sighed deeply. "Bond. James Bond."

"Figures."

The headphones crackled to life, and Oz and D. B. both jumped.

"It's Dupont!" came B-Nut's excited cry, instantly wiping all thoughts of Agent 007 out of Oz's head.

"Where?" Bunsen and Glory asked at the same time.

"Just coming out of the Chinatown exit at Gallery Place. And there must be hundreds—whoa, make that thousands!—of rats on his tail. No pun intended. This could be bigger than we thought."

"I'll alert the Mouse Guard," said Bunsen crisply. "We may have to fly in reinforcements from Annapolis. Glory, Oz, D. B., are you ready?"

"Affirmative," they answered.

"They're moving down Seventh Street," reported B-Nut. "Once Dupont makes the turn onto F, the rats will head straight for the museum."

"Get ready," said Bunsen, his voice squeaking slightly with tension. Oz and D. B. stepped out to the curb.

"Rounding the corner—you should see them any second," B-Nut reported.

"Get set!" said Bunsen.

"There they are!" cried Glory.

As the rats advanced down F Street, led by a swaggering Roquefort Dupont, pandemonium broke loose in front of the museum. Taxis and limousines screeched to a stop. Brakes squealed. Cars honked. Costumed guests and bystanders screamed.

"What the—" D. B.'s mother swiveled around and shaded her eyes against the glare of the headlights. "Holy smokes!" she cried. "Camera! I need a camera on the double!"

The Channel 12 news crew came running. They stopped in their tracks when they saw the rats.

Oz and D. B. stepped into the street.

"Delilah Bean, you get back here this instant!" D. B.'s mother called.

"Just keep walking," said Oz.

"Delilah Bean, do you hear me?"

"Keep walking, just a few more steps."

"Delilah Bean, I'm warning you!"

"I am so grounded," groaned the back end of the Trojan Horse as D. B. ignored her mother and moved reluctantly forward.

Oz stopped and faced the tide of oncoming rats. The rodents slowed at the sight of the unusual four-legged creature, and the back of Oz's neck prickled in revulsion. Never in his life had he imagined there could be so many rats. The street was paved with them, thousands of small furry bodies that advanced in one massive pack, like a fur carpet shuffling down the street. Thousands of hairy snouts pointed in his direction, sniffing the air. Thousands of eyes glowed red at him in the stalled traffic's headlights. Oz tried not to think about what it would feel like to have all those rodents crawling over his body. Those sharp claws! Those long, hairless tails! He shuddered.

"The name is Levinson, Oz Levinson," he whispered to himself, trying to bolster his faltering courage.

"How's it look?" asked D. B.

"You don't want to know."

"Oh, man," his classmate wailed. "I can't even see anything and I'm scared out of my wits."

"Steady now, children," said a voice through their headphones. It was Julius. "Have courage."

The elder mouse's voice was calm and even, and somehow just knowing he was there made Oz feel better. He forced himself to breathe deeply.

"Ready with the net?" asked Bunsen.

"Affirmative," Oz replied.

"Gym bag?"

"Got it," said D. B.

"Now!" cried Glory, leaping out from her hiding place inside one of the donkey's ears. She stood on the Trojan Horse's forehead and cupped her paws around her mouth.

"Hey, Dupont!" she called. "Roquefort Dupont!"

Dupont stopped in his tracks. Scurvy and Gnaw tripped over his tail and tumbled to the ground behind him. "Idiots," growled Dupont. The wave of rats halted.

"Up here!" Glory waved.

Dupont lifted his mangy snout into the air and bared his sharp yellow teeth. "Well if it isn't little Glory Goldenleaf," he snarled. "What a pleasant surprise."

Glory tossed a small ball of yarn over the side of the donkey costume and rappelled neatly down onto the toe of Oz's tennis shoe.

"Steady," said Bunsen in his ear. "Hold your position."

Oz held his position—and his breath. Out of the corner of the Trojan Horse's eyehole he could just make out Glory's tiny form planted defiantly on his shoe. Bunsen was right about her—she was incredibly brave. Especially in the face of an enemy like Roquefort Dupont, who was easily the biggest rat Oz had ever seen.

"What's he look like?" said D. B. tensely.

"Not good," Oz whispered. "Huge. Nearly as big as a cat. And he has red eyes and sharp yellow teeth and—"

"Sorry I asked," muttered D. B.

Oz continued to stare through the eyehole at Dupont. He remembered what Glory had said about him—that he was evil, and mean, and really, really scary. There was no arguing with that.

"You want me?" cried Glory, not a quiver of fear audible in her small mouse voice. "Come and get me!"

"I believe I'll do just that," said Dupont, and took a step forward. "There's no escaping the Black Paw, remember?"

"Hold your ground!" whispered Bunsen. "Steady!"

Without warning, Roquefort Dupont lowered his head and charged. He was surprisingly fast in spite of his bulk, and he covered the few feet of ground between him and Glory in less time than Oz would have thought possible.

Oz almost missed him. Almost.

At the very last second, he whipped the fishing net out from under the donkey costume and brought it whooshing down on Dupont. The rat shrieked with rage as its mesh entangled him. Just as quickly, Oz whipped the net back under the Trojan Horse costume, whisking Dupont out of his followers' view.

Scurvy and Gnaw blinked in surprise. The mass of rats behind them hesitated, confused.

Inside the costume, all was chaos. It was all Oz could do to hang onto the net. Dupont bucked and snarled, thrashing and clawing at the trap. Oz gripped the handle in his left hand, and with his right struggled to hold the top of the net tightly shut.

"You'll pay for this," rasped Dupont.

Oz gasped in shock. He dropped the net.

"Oz!" cried D. B. in dismay.

Somehow, Oz hadn't expected the rodent to speak to him. Hearing Glory and her friends talk was one thing, but coming from Dupont it was nothing short of terrifying.

Dupont gave a triumphant cry and redoubled his efforts to disentangle himself. As he scrabbled toward the opening in the mesh, Oz dropped to his knees and lunged for the net's handle. Dupont slashed at him with his sharp claws and fangs.

"GET OUT OF MY WAY!" the rat howled.

Sweat poured from Oz as he struggled frantically to regain his hold on the fishing net. He couldn't let Dupont get away. Not now. Not after all their efforts.

"Gotcha!" he said, finally scooping the net up again.

"Hang on, Oz!" Glory called, scrambling up his pant leg to safety.

"I'm trying," Oz replied through clenched teeth. "But you'd better hurry."

Outside the costume, Oz could hear the clicking of thousands of rat claws against the pavement as the mass of rodents shifted uneasily in the street.

"Where'd he go?" he heard Gnaw ask.

"Beats me," Scurvy replied.

"I'M IN HERE, YOU IDIOTS!" screamed Dupont.

Oz quickly swung the net against the fabric to muffle his voice.

A rat snout poked under the bottom hem of the costume and snuffled suspiciously at Oz's feet. It was Gnaw. "Boss? Was that you?"

Oz felt rat whiskers brush against his ankle. He felt a rat snout venture up under his pant leg. Oz panicked.

"Run, D. B.!" he cried. "Run!"

"No, Oz!" shouted Glory. "Stop!"

He ignored her and took off toward the museum, dragging D. B. stumbling behind him. The mob of rats shuffled uncertainly forward. They were still confused, but they had caught the sharp scent of fear, and it excited them.

"You know our orders!" shouted Gnaw. "SWARM AND SURROUND!"

Oz ran faster than he had ever run before in his life. He ran blindly, feverishly, charging forward without even bothering to look through the costume's eyeholes. All he could think about was Dupont's wall of horrors. Were his own ears destined to be added to the rat leader's trophies? He gripped the fishing net tightly as he ran, and it flapped rhythmically against the wire mesh framework of the costume, Dupont grunting with each step that he took.

Oz ran fast, but it wasn't fast enough.

In a flash, the rat mob had him surrounded. Oz turned this way and that. He was lathered in sweat and breathing hard.

"Let—me—THROUGH!" He spat the words out, but to no avail. No matter which direction he turned, his feet encountered a mass of furry bodies. Finally, he stopped, panting. His shoulders sagged. It was hopeless. "Sorry, D. B.," he whispered. "Sorry, Glory."

"Don't give up yet," Glory urged. "Hank, B-Nut, you're on!"

At Glory's command, Hank swooped low toward the mass of rodents. B-Nut leaned over his wing and flipped a switch on a small box that hung from pigeon's neck.

"Me, Roquefort Dupont!" boomed a voice from the hearing aid amplifier inside. "The descendant of kings!"

Thousands of rats looked up at the sky, baffled. In the glare of the headlights, they could only see the silhouette of a pigeon. Not a rodent moved, except Dupont, who was still struggling mightily to escape from the fishing net.

"I can't hold on much longer," Oz said grimly. He shot a worried glance at Glory. Had his moment of panic messed things up completely? What if Dupont's followers didn't take the bait?

"Just another second or two," Glory whispered encouragingly. "Bunsen's been splicing tape all afternoon from the dog-doo transmitter feed. It's brilliant."

Hank and B-Nut buzzed back and forth over the mass of rats. "Those mice think they can outwit me, but I'll show them who's boss!" cried the recording. "My ancestors kept mice as servants! I am Roquefort Dupont!"

"It's the Boss!" Scurvy shouted. "The pigeon's got the Boss! GET THAT BIRD!"

At this, Hank flapped off away from the museum—enticingly low, so that the rats would think they stood a chance. Led by Scurvy and Gnaw, the entire mass of rats shifted direction, moving away from the Trojan

Horse that contained Oz and D. B. Picking up speed, they began to chase after Hank. People crowded out of their cars and taxis and limousines to watch. Partygoers flocked to the curb, open-mouthed at the sight of a mob of rodents in pursuit of a pigeon. Dupont's recorded shrieks could be heard echoing in the distance long after pigeon, pilot, and Washington's entire rat population rounded the corner of F Street and disappeared from view.

"I do not believe I just saw that," said D. B.'s mother. "Did we get that on film?"

"Well done," Oz heard Julius exclaim jubilantly over his headphones. "Well done, indeed."

Oz could feel Glory bouncing excitedly up and down on his shoulder. If he hadn't still been clinging to the fishing net so tightly, he would have felt like bouncing himself. Glory turned toward D. B. "Ready?" she cried.

D. B. held up the open gym bag in response.

"Now!" Glory ordered, and in one lightning movement Oz jerked the net toward the bag and dumped Dupont inside. D. B. zipped it shut, instantly muffling the rat's furious snarls. Now it was her turn to hold on for dear life.

"You've gotta help me, Oz," she said desperately, as

Dupont thrashed and pummeled at the bag. "He's going to get away."

Sure enough, just then Dupont managed to slice through the fabric of the bag. An enormous, dingy paw appeared and scrabbled frantically for freedom. Oz reached over to stuff the paw back inside, and the rat slashed at him with his sharp claws.

"Ow!" cried Oz, drawing his hand back in pain. He grabbed the fishing net angrily and swatted at the paw with the handle. Hard. Dupont roared with rage. Oz gave the bag another whack, and the paw withdrew.

"Take that, Roquefort Dupont!" said D. B., the back end of the Trojan Horse wagging as she did a little victory dance. "Take that, rats! You don't know who you're dealing with!"

"I'll tell the Mouse Guard to stand down," said Bunsen. "Oz, you and D. B. deliver the prisoner. Glory, slip away as soon as you can and meet me at the next rendezvous."

If the Trojan Horse seemed a bit more frisky as it made its way through the crowd—Dupont was still putting up a struggle inside the gym bag, albeit a more subdued one, thanks to repeated swats with the fishing net handle—no one said a word. The bystanders were too busy babbling about the rats.

Oz and D. B. ducked around the corner of the museum onto Ninth Street. Dumbarton Goldenleaf stepped out of the shadows. "Good job, kids," he said. "We'll take it from here."

D. B. set the gym bag on the sidewalk and Oz, still nursing his wounded hand, gave it a final thwack for good measure. A team of Mouse Guard commandos materialized and formed a circle around the wriggling bag. They waited for General Goldenleaf's command, then hefted it onto their brawny shoulders. Oz watched as the mice spirited the gym bag down the street toward the museum's employee entrance.

"Mission accomplished," he said to D. B. He turned his head to where Glory still stood perched on his shoulder. "Sorry I almost messed up."

"Never mind about that, Oz. Every spy almost messes up now and then," she assured him. "Look at me. I'm a prime example! But the important thing is, we did it!"

Oz grinned. "We did, didn't we?"

As they trotted back around the corner of the building, D. B.'s mother spotted them. "Delilah Bean, what in tarnation is going on?" she demanded.

D. B. shrugged, and the back end of the Trojan Horse twitched again. "I have absolutely no idea, Mom."

"You kids better get inside," said her mother. "There's something strange going on in this city tonight."

"You think that was strange?" whispered Oz to D. B. as they moved inside. "Just wait. It ain't over till the fat lady sings."

CHAPTER 24

DAY THREE—
SUNDAY
1930 HOURS

Upstairs on the second floor of the Spy Museum, the Halloween party was in full swing.

Twinkling lights had been strung around the mezzanine windows, in front of which stood a row of tables covered in white linen cloths. Clusters of costumed partygoers gathered nearby, plucking appetizers from silver trays and talking in excited voices about what they had just witnessed outside. Others leaned over the railing and gazed down into the lobby, where a huge papier-mâché pumpkin had been placed over the statue of Feliks Dzerzhinsky's head. The museum was gussied up to the gills, with black and silver streamers hanging from the ceilings and real pumpkins scattered here and there, along with scarecrows sporting sunglasses and trenchcoats.

From inside the ballroom could be heard the lively strains of a jazz combo bopping its way through a medley of famous spy theme songs.

"Do you see them?" whispered D. B.

The Trojan Horse's head wagged back and forth as Oz scanned the crowd for Jordan and Tank. He spotted his father ladling punch into a cup for D. B.'s mother. Behind her, the Channel 12 camera crew wandered through the costumed crowd, looking for famous faces.

"No," he said. "They're not out here. Must be in the ballroom."

They trotted slowly forward through the doors. The music grew louder. Again, Oz scanned the room, a little more anxiously this time. What if Jordan and Tank had gone home or snuck off into the exhibits?

"There they are," Oz reported in relief. "By the car."

"Perfect," said D. B. "Knew they couldn't resist the Aston Martin."

The DB5 had been moved into the ballroom for the party. Enthroned on a pedestal in the center of the room, it revolved slowly under the disco ball. Inside, a scarecrow in a tuxedo gripped the wheel. Outside, Tank and Jordan were practically glued to its gleaming silver hood.

"Target in range," Oz said crisply into his microphone. "We're going in."

"Okay, kids, it's time to rock and roll," Glory replied. "Good luck."

The Trojan Horse stepped onto the dance floor. All around them, couples were swaying to the strains of "Secret Agent Man."

"Let's make this good," said Oz.

"I'm behind you all the way," D. B. replied with a nervous snort of laughter. "Get it? *Behind?*"

"Pathetic," said Oz, but he smiled anyway.

Slowly at first, and then with a little more assurance, Oz and D. B. began to dance. They tried to stay in tandem as they kicked out first one leg and then the other, moving their hips and shoulders to the beat. All the while, they were drawing closer to the car.

"Oh look, the Trojan Horse is dancing!" cried the woman dressed as Emma Peel. She was shimmying with her bald James Bond. "How cute!"

"She won't think it's so cute if the Trojan Horse kicks her," muttered D. B.

"Hang on, D. B.," said Oz. "We're almost there."

As the song came to an end, the Trojan Horse lowered its head. "The name is Levinson, Oz Levinson," murmured Oz, and he charged straight at Jordan and Tank, ramming them with his full weight. His

classmates' legs flew out from under them and they landed in a heap on the floor.

"Watch it!" cried Tank angrily.

Neither Oz nor D. B. said a word. Oz turned away, and D. B. swung her shoulders from side to side. The Trojan Horse's rear end wagged tauntingly at the two boys.

"Who's in there, anyway?" demanded Jordan, scrambling to his feet and brushing off his tuxedo. He peered into one of the eyeholes.

"Hey, I know those sneakers," said Tank, pointing at D. B.'s feet. D. B. stuck out a skinny leg and waved a red tennis shoe at them.

"Dogbones!" said Jordan in disgust. "Dogbones and Fatboy. I should have known."

Oz and D. B. trotted slowly forward, circling the sports car. The band had swung into the theme song from *Mission: Impossible* and the dancers drew back to make room for the costumed creature.

"Where do you think you're going?" called Jordan. "Get back here!"

Oz and D. B. ignored him and kept trotting around the Aston Martin. Jordan raced after them. As Oz came around the other side, he stopped short. Tank stood in front of him, blocking the way. His arms were crossed over his beefy chest. He'd doubled back and cut them off.

"Nowhere to run, Fatboy," he said, wagging his golden finger at them.

"Yeah," added Jordan, panting as he caught up. "You two losers are in for it now."

The music was still playing, but the partygoers closest to them had stopped dancing. Out of the corner of one of the eyeholes, Oz saw Mrs. Busby enter the ballroom. She frowned when she spotted Jordan and Tank.

"I think it's time Double-O-Lard here did a little dance just for us," said Jordan.

"Dance or run," echoed Tank. "Which is it going to be?"

Oz couldn't see them, but he knew that up above, all along the exposed pipes that ran across the ceiling, Julius and the rest of the mice were watching him. "I'm booking balcony seats," Julius had joked yesterday after Glory described her plan. "Wouldn't miss this for the world."

Oz wasn't alone anymore. He had friends. Brave, loyal friends. And for the first time in a long time he didn't wish he were invisible. In fact, he was downright glad everyone could see him. He was never going to slip under the radar again. He was Oz Levinson, secret agent.

Conqueror of Roquefort Dupont. Rescuer of spy mice.

Reaching up, he removed the donkey head. "I'm not going to run," he said quietly.

"Dance then, Fatboy," said Jordan.

Oz didn't move.

"I said dance!"

"My name," Oz said slowly and carefully, "is not Fatboy." He glanced upward. He hoped that Julius could hear him. "My name is Ozymandias."

"And besides, it's the fat *lady* you need to watch out for," added D. B., wriggling out from underneath the rear end of the costume.

"What fat lady?" said Tank, looking around.

Oz smiled. "The one who's about to SING!"

As soon as Oz shouted the word "sing," Glory and Bunsen shot out from their hiding place under the Aston Martin. Glory ran up Jordan's pant leg; Bunsen ran up Tank's.

For a moment, time stood still. Oz and D. B. waited, both of them smiling broadly in anticipation. And then Jordan began to jerk his tuxedoed leg frantically back and forth.

"What the—get it OUT!" he cried.

Tank's eyes widened in terror as Bunsen scampered up and down inside his pants. He opened his mouth, but nothing came out. He began to hop wildly from one leg to the other and finally emitted a high-pitched shriek.

The mice moved up inside the boys' shirts. Jordan and Tank began twitching their arms and slapping at themselves, but Glory and Bunsen were far too fast for them. Up and down through their clothes the mice ran, and up and down jumped Jordan and Tank, gyrating wildly.

"Nice moves, boys!" called someone from the crowd, and the partygoers started clapping to the music.

"What do you call that dance, son?" cried an elderly Supreme Court justice dressed as the Pink Panther.

"Looks like the jerk to me!" said the Julius Caesar.

"More like two jerks!" called D. B., and the crowd hooted.

Frantic by now, Jordan scrambled up onto the hood of the James Bond car.

"Go, Double-O-Seven!" shouted someone behind them, as he twitched and shook and slapped at his clothes. Tank was rolling on the floor at this point, close to tears.

As the band swung into the familiar "dun-duhduh-dun-dun" opening notes of the James Bond theme song, the car's headlights switched on and the gun ports flipped open, emitting sharp bursts of light. The delighted crowd began to cheer.

Oz and D. B. slapped each other a high five.

"Are you getting this?" D. B.'s mother called excitedly to her camera crew.

Herbie, the museum security guard, began to make his way through the crowd. "You kids get down off there!" he called.

Just as he reached the revolving podium, in one last desperate attempt to rid himself of his unseen tormentor, Jordan Scott pulled down his pants. The crowd exploded with laughter. In the confusion, Oz saw Glory scoot out from one pant leg and vanish again under the car.

"Nice boxers!" someone shouted.

Jordan Scott quickly crouched down, but not before the crowd—and the cameras—got a good look at his underpants. Big, baggy, bright red underpants. Almost as red as Jordan's face. They were covered with large white hearts, inside of which were the words "Hot Stuff."

Herbie grabbed him by the collar and yanked him off the Aston Martin. "Come on, Hot Stuff," he said in disgust. "Party's over."

"They're my dad's," mumbled Jordan as he and Tank were hustled out of the ballroom. "They were the only ones that were clean."

As the excitement died down and the music picked up again, Luigi Levinson and Amelia Bean approached their children.

"I do not believe I just saw that," said D. B.'s mother.

"What was that all about?" asked Oz's father.

D. B. looked at Oz. Oz looked at D. B. They grinned and slapped each other a high five.

Oz turned to the grown-ups. "I think you could say that the fat lady just sang."

CHAPTER 25

DAY THREE
SUNDAY
2200 HOURS

"Strange happenings in down-town D. C. tonight," announced D. B.'s mother from the TV screen.

Oz and D. B. were back at Oz's house, sitting in the living room, eating chocolate chip cookies and watching the ten o'clock news.

Onscreen, Amelia Bean stared soberly into the camera as footage of the rat mob appeared on the screen behind her. "Wildlife experts at the National Zoo say it must have been the influence of the full moon that caused rats to flood the streets of our nation's capital this evening. A masquerade party at the International Spy Museum was briefly interrupted by the commotion, but in an amazing twist of events, an unlikely pied piper in the form of a pigeon led the rodents away."

D. B. hoisted her glass of milk at the screen in a

toast. "Go, B-Nut and Hank!" she said.

"The rats charted a course through the heart of downtown and ended up at the Tidal Basin. They were last seen swimming toward the Potomac. Meanwhile, city officials interviewed by Channel Twelve hastened to assure the public that the Metro is still safe to ride. An extermination team will be working through the night inspecting all lines and subway cars to ensure a smooth commute by tomorrow morning."

"Bingo," said Oz softly. He glanced down at the tiny object in his hand. It wasn't anything special, really, just a gold button foraged from a navy blazer left in the Spy Museum's lost-and-found. The Spy Mice Agency logo had been etched onto the front of it, and a small safety pin was glued to the back. Oz was proud to have it all the same.

"Honorary field agents for the Spy Mice Agency," he said, holding it up to the light. "I still can't believe Julius gave us these."

"Me neither," said D. B., admiring hers as well.

Espionage, Julius had told them a short while ago in a solemn ceremony down at Checkpoint Charlie, was a shadowy business.

"It's not always possible to publicly thank those who have served courageously," he explained. "If word got out that the Mouse Code has been broken, and that our agency has had contact with humans, it could create chaos throughout the Guilds. The Council must never know." He waved a paw at Glory, Bunsen, B-Nut, and the Steel Acorns. "But we all know, and we won't forget. And we also know how to find you if we ever need you again."

At this, Glory had winked at them both and tapped the phone booth door with her elegant little paw. "Dead drop," she whispered.

Oz's father poked his head in from the kitchen. "What do you two little pumpkin pies have there?" he asked curiously.

Oz and D. B. hastily pocketed their badges of honor. "Nothing, Dad. Just some leftover Halloween candy from the party," Oz replied.

"Say, isn't that your classmate?" said his father, pointing at the television.

Sure enough, as footage of Jordan's wild dance atop the Aston Martin appeared, Amelia Bean's voice-over continued: "On the lighter side, there were more strange happenings in the city tonight. During the Spy Museum's popular 'Come as Your Favorite Spy' masquerade party, two students from the Chester B. Arthur Elementary School seemed more intent on *un*dressing than on dressing up."

The camera caught Tank rolling on the floor, then zoomed in for a close-up of Jordan Scott's boxer shorts. Oz started to laugh. It would be a long time before the sharks lived that one down.

His father gave a rueful smile. "Poor kids," he said. "How embarrassing! Though from what Mrs. Busby told me, they deserved it. Do you know one of the caterers found a gym bag from your school just inside the Ninth Street employee entrance? There was a rat inside, of all things! Those two troublemakers must have been planning to cause a ruckus."

Oz and D. B. exchanged a guilty glance.

"What happened to the rat, Dad?" asked Oz.

"Scared the caterer so badly he dropped the bag," Luigi Levinson continued, shaking his head. "Along with a tray of stuffed mushrooms. The rat ran for the door. Probably down at the river right now, skinny-dipping with all his friends." Still shaking his head, he left the room.

"So Dupont escaped," mused D. B.

Oz reached into his pocket and pulled out the button badge. "Somehow I don't think we've seen the last of that slimy rodent," he said, tracing the Spy Mice Agency insignia—a mouse in dark glasses—with his fingertip. "Not by a long shot."

CHAPTER 26

DAY THREE
SUNDAY
22:15 HOURS

Back at the Spy Mice Agency,
the party was winding down.

Only a few mice remained on
the dance floor, swaying to the sweet
strains of "That Old Mouse Magic." The Steel Acorns
had rocked the crowd to their hard-driving beat earlier
in the evening as the jubilant mice celebrated their victory over the rats. Now, however, the band was in a
more mellow mood. Onstage, B-Nut crooned the words
to the familiar melody, eyes closed and tail swishing
gently back and forth to the music's slow rhythm.
Behind him, Lip and Romeo strummed their electric
guitars, while Nutmeg kept time by drawing a pastry
brush lightly over his drum set's cymbals (foraged soup
can lids).

The Foragers had gone all out to help transform

the space under the Spy City Café floor into a breathtaking ballroom. A handsome silk scarf (found under one of the restaurant's booths) had been tacked to the ceiling in loose billows, giving the spacious room the look of an exotic tent. Tinsel (salvaged from a recycled Christmas tree) had been draped along the walls, and hundreds of birthday candles were clustered on tables made from animal cracker boxes covered with bright scraps of wrapping paper. A disco ball had even been fashioned by gluing silver sequins to an old tennis ball. It twirled slowly from the string that held it to the ceiling, shimmering in the candlelight.

On the far side of the room, Julius sat on a sofa made from a sponge covered with a piece of velvet. He was deep in conversation with several Council members and Dumbarton Goldenleaf. Next to the general sat a glowing Gingersnap Goldenleaf, her husband's paw clasped tightly in her own.

The song came to an end, and Gingersnap yawned. "We should be getting home soon," she whispered. "The last pigeons will be leaving soon, and I need to check on Truffle and Taffy."

Her husband patted her cheek fondly. "Just a few more minutes, dear," he said. "I'm sure our babies are fine. Blueberry and Pumpkin will have everything under control."

Fumble trundled by just then, pushing a small cart (half of an eyeglasses case outfitted with wheels foraged from broken inline skates). Julius, who was not entirely convinced that his stout staff member had acted innocently in squealing on Bunsen and Glory, had assigned Fumble to cleanup crew as punishment.

Glory, who was seated next to her mother, saluted him with her punch cup.

"Cheers," she said.

Fumble didn't reply.

"You missed a pile of sunflower seeds someone spilled over there," said Glory helpfully, pointing toward the stage. Her colleague glared at her, seemed about to say something, then slumped and trundled on.

Glory smiled and took a sip of strawberry punch. She twitched her elegant little nose. The bubbles from the ginger ale in the mixture tickled. Then she yawned. It had been a very long evening. A wonderful evening, but a very long one.

Someone cleared his throat. She looked up to see Bunsen standing in front of her. He'd cleaned off the shoe polish, and his fur gleamed snowy white again in the candlelight. The tip of his nose was as pink as the punch. Glory peered at it and frowned. "Are you coming down with something?" she asked her colleague.

"Me?" squeaked Bunsen.

"Your nose," said Glory. "It's all pink."

Bunsen hastily covered it with his paw. "Oh, that," he said. "Uh, well—"

Gingersnap Goldenleaf leaned over to her daughter. "He's blushing, you goose," she whispered in Glory's ear. "Probably wants to ask you to dance. Put the poor fellow out of his misery."

Now it was Glory's turn to blush. "Oh," she said. She handed her punch cup to her mother and stood up. "Would you like to dance?"

The slim white lab mouse nodded. Holding out his paw, he led Glory out onto the dance floor as the Steel Acorns struck up the opening bars of "Whiskers in the Moonlight." Bunsen shyly wrapped his paw around Glory's waist and pulled her close. They began to sway to the music.

"Glory, I—"

"Wasn't this an amazing day?" said Glory.

Bunsen glanced down at Glory, who had pressed her furry cheek close to his. "Truly amazing," he said.

"Did you ever dream something like this could happen?"

"Mmm-hmmm," murmured Bunsen, closing his eyes. "Often." He began to hum.

Glory drew back. "You did?"

Her colleague's eyes flew open. "Oh, I mean, uh—no! Never!" Bunsen cleared his throat. "Unbelievable!"

Glory smiled and snuggled close again. "I know, isn't it?" she continued. "We got the Kiss of Death back, and we got my father back—and I got my job back!" she said happily.

"And don't forget your Silver Skateboard," added Bunsen.

Glory glanced over at the far wall, against which she'd propped her shiny new skateboard. "Oh, I won't, believe me," she said, sighing in contentment. "Truly an amazing day. And to top it all off, we foiled Operation P.E.S.T. Control! Though it's a shame Dupont escaped from the Mouse Guard." She pulled away again. "Oh, I almost forgot!"

"What?" said her colleague.

"You got promoted, Bunsen. Congratulations!" Glory held out her paw.

Bunsen shook it, ducking his head modestly. "That certainly was a surprise," he said. "I never dreamed—

never expected—well, you know, being just a lab mouse and all . . ."

"Just a lab mouse?" cried Glory. "Bunsen, you are true blue. And besides, you should never be ashamed of who you are!" A rueful smile flickered across her face at these words, and her bright little eyes flew over to where her boss sat, still talking to her father. Good old Julius. Glory hesitated a moment, then confided, "You know, I'm half house mouse myself."

There. She'd said it. The sky hadn't fallen in. The world hadn't come to an end.

"Oh, I know that," said Bunsen.

"You do?" Glory blinked at him.

"Sure, everybody knows that. Besides, it's a nice half." Bunsen's nose and the tip of his tail turned bright pink again. "Of course, I like your other half too. In fact," he finished boldly, "I like everything about you."

"Oh my," said Glory. She stared at Bunsen. For once she was speechless.

Bunsen pulled her close again and began to hum along to the music once more. Glory's face wore a thoughtful expression as they spun into a slow waltz. Across the room, Gingersnap Goldenleaf watched as the two of them dipped and twirled. She smiled and squeezed her husband's paw. B-Nut grinned and waved from the stage. Julius regarded the young couple pensively, stroking his whiskers. And the sequined tennis ball that hung from the ceiling above cast a shower of sparkling light over them all as the two mice danced off across the ballroom floor.